This book is published under the auspices of

THE WINSCROFT FOUNDATION

... established in 1972 to provide initiation ...
... research, diagnosis and treatment of eye diseases.

Examples of contributions made are:

A.C.   Initiated Assessment Unit at
        Moorfield's Hospital, London

        T valuoperation team, in the
        Western Ophthalmic Hospital, London

        M. Chair of Ophthalmology at the
        University of Leicester.

The establishment of a Royal Australian College
of Ophthalmologists Fellowship.

You can help, in however small a way, continue
by making a donation but leaving a legacy. However
small the amount, no matter how small is received
with gratitude. Please write for details to:

THE WINSCROFT FOUNDATION

The Green, Tredegar Road, Anstey,
Leicester LE7 7FU, England.
Telephone: (0116) 236 4123.

In Australia write to:

THE WINSCROFT FOUNDATION

c/o The Royal Australian College of
Ophthalmologists,
27, Commonwealth Street, Sydney,
N.S.W., 2010.

SPECIAL MESSAGE TO READERS

This book is published under the auspices of

THE ULVERSCROFT FOUNDATION

(registered charity No. 264873 UK)

Established in 1972 to provide funds for research, diagnosis and treatment of eye diseases. Examples of contributions made are: —

A new Children's Assessment Unit at Moorfield's Hospital, London.

•

Twin operating theatres at the Western Ophthalmic Hospital, London.

•

A Chair of Ophthalmology at the University of Leicester.

•

The establishment of a Royal Australian College of Ophthalmologists "Fellowship".

You can help further the work of the Foundation by making a donation or leaving a legacy. Every contribution, no matter how small, is received with gratitude. Please write for details to:

**THE ULVERSCROFT FOUNDATION,
The Green, Bradgate Road, Anstey,
Leicester LE7 7FU, England.
Telephone: (0116) 236 4325**

**In Australia write to:
THE ULVERSCROFT FOUNDATION,
c/o The Royal Australian College of
Ophthalmologists,
27, Commonwealth Street, Sydney,
N.S.W. 2010.**

COOGAN'S QUEST

Coogan came down from Wyoming on the trail of a man he had vowed to kill — Red Sheene, known as The Butcher. But Sheene proved difficult to run to earth, for he and his gang had a secret hideaway into which they vanished after carrying out their evil crimes. It was the kidnap of Marian De Quincey that gave Coogan his chance — but he was to need help from an unexpected quarter to avoid losing his own life.

J. P. WESTON

COOGAN'S QUEST

Complete and Unabridged

LINFORD
Leicester

First published in Great Britain in 1992 by
Robert Hale Limited
London

First Linford Edition
published 1997
by arrangement with
Robert Hale Limited
London

The right of J. P. Weston to be identified as
the author of this work has been asserted by
him in accordance with the
Copyright, Designs and Patents Act, 1988

British Library CIP Data

Weston, J. P.
  Coogan's quest.—Large print ed.—
Linford western library
1. English fiction- -20th century
2. Large type books
I. Title
823.9'14 [F]

ISBN 0–7089–5051–5

Published by
F. A. Thorpe (Publishing) Ltd.
Anstey, Leicestershire

Set by Words & Graphics Ltd.
Anstey, Leicestershire
Printed and bound in Great Britain by
T. J. Press (Padstow) Ltd., Padstow, Cornwall

This book is printed on acid-free paper

1

COOGAN heard the shouting and the laughter as he rode up the trail. The sound appeared to be coming from behind some large boulders just up ahead. Then came a scream undoubtedly uttered by a woman. But the laughter was certainly male; it sounded coarse and evil; not at all pleasant to hear.

Coogan checked his horse, eased himself out of the saddle and tethered the animal to a stunted bush growing by the side of the trail. He lifted the Winchester rifle out of its bucket and moved softly towards the boulders. A narrow gap between two of them gave him a view of what lay on the other side. There the ground dropped away to a saucer-shaped depression, the trail following the bend of the rim on the left.

In this hollow lay the wreck of a one-horse covered wagon of the type used by itinerant traders. It appeared to have swerved off the trail and fallen down the steepest part of the depression, and it was now lying on its side with two of the wheels smashed. The horse was still harnessed to it, but one of the shafts was broken and the animal was dead.

There was a dead man, too; grey-haired and bearded. Even at a distance it was apparent that he had been shot in the head, and he was lying face-upward on the bare stony ground, staring sightlessly at the clear blue sky above him.

These basic facts Coogan took in at a glance; also the presence of three saddled horses tethered in a group on the right. But what really seized his attention was the action that was taking place in the centre of the hollow like a scene from a melodrama.

There were three men and a woman taking part. The men were evil-looking

2

characters, stubbly-chinned, sweaty-shirted, wearing gun-belts; and they seemed to be using the woman as a kind of human toy which they were passing from one to another, each of them tearing off a piece of her clothing while the other two looked on gloatingly, yelling encouragement and taunting the victim. Already she was half-naked and it was only too apparent how the play would end if they had their way.

Coogan knew that it was none of his business and that a man could make a load of trouble for himself by stepping into other people's affairs. Undoubtedly the sensible thing to do would be to go back to his horse, hoist himself into the saddle, make a wide detour round the hollow and ride on. That way he would not become involved in something that was certainly no concern of his.

It took him precisely two seconds to decide not to do the sensible thing. Instead he levered a round into the breech of the Winchester, took careful aim and fired a shot into the ground a few inches to the left of the man who was taking his turn with the woman. The bullet kicked up a little spurt of dust and the crack of the gun startled all three of them. Their heads jerked round like animated puppets in the direction from which the report had come.

"Let her go," Coogan said sharply.

He was visible to them in the V-shaped opening between the boulders and they could see the rifle pointing at them, threatening.

For a moment nobody moved; it was as though this abrupt intervention of another person had frozen them where they stood. Then the one who was holding the woman released her and reached for his gun. The woman, finding herself unexpectedly free, had the good sense to make a run for it. She scuttered away like a scared rabbit, taking herself out of the line of fire.

The man was still hauling his weapon clear of the leather when Coogan shot him in the chest. He did it with cold precision like someone carrying out an execution, and he had another round in the breech of the repeater before either of the other men could draw a bead on him. The second man met the same fate as the first; his legs folded and he dropped to the ground and did not get up.

Only the third man succeeded in firing a shot in reply to Coogan's attack, and this flew wide, hitting one of the boulders and ricochetting away with an angry screech. Coogan shot him in the right forearm and he let out a yell and dropped his gun.

Coogan stepped through the gap and came down into the hollow, Winchester in hand. The two dead men lay where they had fallen, soundless, motionless, out of it all. The wounded man was clutching his right arm and blood was dripping from the hand; his mouth was twisted in a grimace of pain. Coogan walked up to him and kicked the revolver away. He peered into the man's face and give a low surprised whistle.

"Well, would you believe! Ben Krane!"

The man stared back at him with venom in his eyes. "Who in hell are you?"

"Don't you know?"

"Damned if I do."

"Too bad," Coogan said. "Where's Sheene?"

"I don't know what you're talking about."

"I'm talking about Red Sheene. Outlaw, bank robber, gang-leader, murderer, filth. Butcher Sheene. You're one of his men. You're filth too."

"I never heard of the man. You're crazy."

Coogan hit him on the side of the jaw with the stock of the rifle and Krane gave a howl.

"Don't fool with me," Coogan said. "I'm not in the mood. They've got your picture pinned up alongside his in sheriffs' offices and suchlike places offering a reward dead or alive. You

6

were with him when he and his hellhounds were running wild to the north of here. You and those two beauties there, I guess." He indicated the dead men with a jerk of the thumb. "They got names?"

"Art Waters and Joe Bradley," Krane answered sullenly. "You made a mistake killing them, mister."

"Somebody should've done it years ago. It won't be bothering me none."

"It should. Make no mistake, you'll pay for it. Sure as hell you will."

"Maybe. So where's Sheene?"

Krane scowled at him but said nothing. He appeared to be in some pain from the wound in his forearm. He sat down suddenly and rested his head on his knees, looking sick.

"Okay," Coogan said. "Wherever he is I'll find him. I'll catch up with him sometime, however long it takes. There's a score to settle."

He left Krane and walked over to where the woman was kneeling beside the grey-haired man. She had raised his head from the ground and had it cradled in her arm as if in the hope that life might yet revive in it. But there was no possibility of that, not after what the bullet had done.

"It's no use," Coogan said. "He's dead."

She glanced up at him. "I know."

He was surprised to see that she was not weeping. Perhaps she figured it was no time for tears; perhaps the tears would come later, in private. She was younger than the man, quite a lot younger, and not at all bad-looking: auburn hair combed back from a broad forehead and tied in a pony-tail at the back of the neck, fine bone structure, nicely shaped nose, generous mouth, skin somewhat darkened by exposure to sun and weather, eyes blue and candid with no hint of deceit in them.

"Your husband?"

"No," she said. "My father."

It was the more likely relationship, bearing in mind the obvious difference in their ages; but some young women married older men. Sometimes it even worked.

"What do I call you?"

"I'm Lois Lloyd."

Coogan volunteered the information he had denied to Krane. "Brad Coogan. What happened?"

"Those men waylaid us. They shot Pa and the wagon went over the edge. They shot the horse too."

"Were they aiming to rob you?"

"I guess so. When they'd had their bit of fun."

She spoke bitterly, and with reason. Coogan could have figured things out for himself; had indeed already done so. The woman, who was in fact no more than a girl, was merely confirming his own conclusions.

"What do you propose doing with your father?"

She gave a hopeless shrug. "Guess I'll have to bury him."

"Look," Coogan said, "there's a town named Pikeville maybe five miles up the trail, and there's two dead villains and

9

a live one I reckon I'll be taking in for the sheriff to deal with. We could take your father along too; there's enough horses. Get him a decent burial."

She seemed to give the suggestion some thought, and Coogan suspected she was torn between the idea of burying the grey-haired man out there where he had met his death and having him put in a cemetery side by side with a lot of strangers, including two of the ruffians who had killed him. But finally she decided to accept the offer.

He gave a nod. "Better be moving then. It'll be dark by the time we reach town."

* * *

They rode into Pikeville in the gathering dusk of evening. It was a curious little cavalcade. Krane's wound had been roughly, and indeed somewhat grudgingly, bandaged with a strip of cloth ripped from his own shirt, and the arm was in a sling made from a

10

piece of blanket. He had lost a lot of blood and was swaying in the saddle.

The girl was mounted up behind Coogan. She had made a quick change from her torn clothing into a shirt and a pair of faded cotton pants taken from the wrecked van, and there were scuffed riding-boots on her feet and a short leather jacket over the shirt. She had packed a few things in an old carpet-bag which was tied to the saddle of the horse that was carrying her father's body. The bodies of the two badmen were slung across the back of the fourth horse.

Pikeville was not much of a town. There was a main street running straight through it like a needle, with clapboard buildings lining it on each side. There were few people around and about, and the latest arrivals attracted less attention than they might have done if they had arrived in broad daylight. It seemed a dead-and-alive sort of place with the only sign of any great activity coming from a saloon on the left where a beam of yellow light flooded out over the top of the batwing doors and a honky-tonk piano could be heard.

About fifty yards farther along they came to the sheriff's office, where Coogan brought his party to a halt and dismounted and tethered his horse to a hitching-rail. He had to help Krane out of the saddle; the man might have fallen otherwise. Then with Krane and the girl following he went into the office, leaving the horses with the three dead bodies outside.

Sheriff Loder appeared startled to see them. A big paunchy man with thinning black hair and a pitted nose, he had been sitting in a wooden armchair tilted back with his feet on the desk in front of him and a corncob pipe stuck in his mouth, taking his ease and evidently not expecting anything in the line of business to disturb him. One look at the two men and the girl must have warned him that he had trouble on his hands. But he spoke affably enough.

12

"Now what can I do for you good people?"

Coogan answered him. "There's three dead men outside I just brought in for burial. Shot."

Loder's eyes narrowed and he took his feet off the desk. "That so? Who shot 'em?"

"I shot two. The third one, this young lady's pa, was shot by that bastard there, assisted by the other two, now deceased."

"Well now," Loder said, "that sounds mighty interestin'." He looked at the girl. "Why'd they shoot your paw?"

She told him briefly. "It was a hold-up. We had this one-horse wagon, a kind of travelling store. Pa was driving. They just rode up and shot him. The wagon ran off the trail into a hollow and broke up."

"And you?"

"I was thrown clear."

"Then what?"

"Then the men got off their horses and assaulted me."

"Assaulted, huh?" Sheriff Loder repeated the word, rolling it round his tongue as though it were an expression he did not use very often. "Assaulted!" His gaze shifted to Coogan. "That where you come in?"

"Yes."

"Just happened along as this here assault was taking place?"

"That's correct. I'd heard the shooting when I was a way down the trail, so I was riding wary. Then I heard men's voices up ahead. There was a lot of shouting and laughing, like they was playing some kinda game. Then there was a woman's voice too, screaming, like she was crying out for help. So I got off my horse and went to have a look-see from behind some rocks, taking my Winchester with me."

"And when you saw what was going on you shot the men? Just like that?"

"No," Coogan said, "not just like that. I warned them first. They went for their guns. What would you have done in my place?"

14

Loder declined to answer that one. He turned again to the girl. "That the way it happened?"

"Yes," she said, "that's the way it happened."

For the first time the sheriff addressed himself to Ben Krane, who was looking sick and had been saying nothing.

"You got anything to say?"

"Sure," Krane mumbled. "It's lies, all lies."

"You didn't shoot this young lady's father?"

"Oh, sure," Krane said. "Me and the others. But only because the old goat fished out a shotgun and started popping off at us. It was self-defence."

"Is this true, ma'am?" Loder asked. "Did your paw loose off at them?"

"Of course he didn't. He just picked up the gun to try and frighten them away."

"You sayin' he didn't fire it?"

"Yes, I am. It wasn't even loaded. He never liked to keep a loaded gun

15

lying around. He was a peace-loving man."

Loder spoke to Krane again. "You heard what the lady said?"

Krane sneered. "I heard. It's about what she would say, ain't it?"

"But you still say it happened the way you told it?"

"You bet I do."

Coogan broke in impatiently. "Look, Sheriff, do we have to go on with this? Anybody can see who's lying. This man's name is Ben Krane; he's a wanted outlaw; one of the Sheene gang."

The information appeared to startle Loder and he gave Krane a closer look. "That so?"

Krane said nothing but there was a kind of smirk on his face as he met the sheriff's gaze.

"Guess you've heard of them?" Coogan said.

"Who hasn't?"

"So don't you think you ought to put this joker behind bars?"

Loder frowned. "I'll make my own decision what to do with him. Looks to me like he could use some attention to that right arm."

"Damn right, I could," Krane said. "I need a doctor. I think I got some broken bones."

"Okay, we'll get Doc Lawson if he's around. But in the meantime I guess it won't do no harm to provide you with a bit of accommodation."

Loder heaved himself up off his chair and took a bunch of keys from a hook on the wall behind him. "You can bunk down in one of the cells."

"You mean you're locking me up?" Krane sounded indignant, a picture of injured innocence.

"Just until we get this business sorted out." Loder spoke almost apologetically, which seemed strange to Coogan. "You won't take no harm in there."

Krane seemed prepared to argue, but it was obvious that he was feeling really sick, and maybe he figured that a bunk to lie on even behind bars was better than nothing in the way of a bed. He gave a shrug of the shoulders and allowed Loder to conduct him to the cells at the rear of the building and lock him in.

When the sheriff came back he said: "I didn't catch your name, mister."

"Been strange if you had," Coogan said. "I didn't mention it."

"You going to mention it now?"

"Brad Coogan. And the lady's name is Lois Lloyd."

Loder nodded. "Can't recall seeing you in town before this, Mr Coogan. You from these parts?"

"No. Up north a fair way. Got me a little spread up there. Correction: had a little spread."

"But not any more?"

"Not any more." Coogan's voice had hardened; his eyes were flinty.

"How come?"

"It's a long story."

"And you're not telling it?"

"No."

It was not such a long story really,

but he had no wish to tell it to this Pikeville sheriff who was not the kind of individual he would ever have had any urge to confide in. The man had not impressed him favourably from the moment he had walked into the office and seen him with his feet up on the desk. There was a certain shiftiness about the eyes, a hint that here was someone not to be fully trusted, someone who might play you a dirty trick if it happened to be in his own interests to do so.

Therefore he did not relate the story of that day when he had returned home from a long journey into the nearest town to find inside the log cabin which he and Maria had built with their own hands a scene of utter destruction, as though a party of madmen had been through the place intent on leaving behind them nothing but the broken pieces of what had been a well-loved home. It was vandalism beyond imagining; a crazy bout of wrecking for no other purpose but the complete ruination of the work of someone else.

Yet this, bad as it was, was by no means the worst of it.

It was the silence that warned him; the brooding silence like a premonition of something too dreadful to reveal itself by any sound. It made him hesitate to go into the bedroom; but he had to do so. The rough unpainted door was slightly ajar; it made a creaking sound which broke the silence as he pushed it open. And then he saw what he had dreaded seeing: his wife's body lying on the torn and bloodstained mattress of the bed. She was naked and mutilated beyond recognition, her face nothing but a ghastly pulp, as if it had been crushed under a succession of frenzied blows. He could only guess what had been done to her before the final killing, but it could not be doubted that they had raped her. How many of them, one after another? Again he could only guess, tormenting himself almost to madness with the thought.

He looked for the child, his five-year-old daughter, Poppy. The search did not take long. She was in a corner of the room under a blanket; dead also, bloodstained also, mutilated also. Had they violated her too, he wondered?

He was blind with rage; he beat the wall with his fist until the knuckles were raw and bleeding, scarcely aware of the pain. He had an impulse to rush out of the cabin, jump on his horse and ride off in pursuit of the men who had committed these atrocities. But he did not know who they were or where they had gone. To set out on such a random chase would have been futile.

Only later did he learn that the Sheene gang had been on the rampage in the area, looting, raping and killing. He learned also that they had headed south. After settling his affairs he had ridden south also, on a mission of vengeance.

But he would not tell Loder this.

He had had it in his mind to kill Ben Krane, as he had killed

Waters and Bradley; in his book any member of the Sheene gang was deserving of execution. But he had stayed his hand because of a feeling that Krane might give him a lead to the gang's whereabouts and to Red Sheene, otherwise known as The Butcher, himself. He had made a vow never to rest until either he or Sheene was dead.

A deputy came into the office, a tall gangling young man. Loder informed Coogan and Miss Lloyd that this was Luke Mackley. The deputy had noticed the horses with their gruesome burdens outside and naturally wanted to know what was going on. Loder told him briefly.

Mackley seemed impressed. "Boy, oh boy!"

"There's a guy in one of the cells needing attention." Loder said. "You better go fetch Doc Lawson, and while you're about it you can tell Zeke Nudds there's business for him."

When Mackley had departed on

his errands Loder volunteered the information that Nudds was the Pikeville undertaker, and in fact it was he who arrived first on the scene. Indeed, he came so promptly that Coogan wondered whether he stayed at his place of business waiting for custom to come his way at any time of the day or night.

Apart from the fact that he was dressed in a rusty black suit, Nudds did not look like an undertaker; he was far too well-nourished and rosy-cheeked. Much though he might try to present a sad and sober aspect, jollity would keep breaking through; it was in the twinkling of his eyes and in the humorous turn of his mouth. It was all too obvious that he enjoyed his work, and perhaps more especially the profit to be gained from it. To him three corpses were just so much grist to the undertaking mill.

Doc Lawson took rather longer to arrive. He was a stout grey-haired character in a loud check suit sprinkled with snuff, who breathed whisky fumes over anyone within range. Apparently he had had to be dug out of a poker game in a back room of the saloon and then had had to go home to pick up his black leather bag.

"So where's the patient?" he demanded, casting a somewhat moist and bloodshot eye around the office. "Which of you is it that requires the benefit of me medical expertise? Lady or gentleman?"

"No one in here, Doc," Loder explained. "He's in a cell."

"In a cell, is it? So it's a piece of criminal scum I've been dragged away from a winning streak to attend to? My God, what are things coming to these days? Well, lead me to him."

He spent very little time with the injured man; no doubt he was eager to get back to his winning streak, if in fact it existed. His verdict was that there were after all no bones broken and that Krane was making a lot of fuss about nothing very much.

"No fear of his dying, more's the

pity. In a few days he'll be well enough to go about his evil business again. That's if he's not booked for the hangman. Looks like a gallows-bird to me."

"He is," Coogan said. "He's one of the Sheene gang."

Doc Lawson gave a low whistle. "Is that a fact? One of the Butcher Boys!" He had evidently heard of Sheene and his crew. "Think of that now."

Zeke Nudds had gone off to root out his assistant and grave-digger, Jerry Mangin, a living skeleton who looked far more suited to the interment trade than the undertaker himself. They arrived with a buckboard as the doctor was leaving and lifted the corpses on to it for conveyance to the funeral parlour down the street.

Lois Lloyd went outside to speak to Nudds about her father's burial and Coogan consulted Sheriff Loder on the question of accommodation, not only for himself but for the girl.

"If you're looking for some place

nice and quiet where the beds are clean and the grub's eatable you can't do better than Mrs Goobey's. Luke will show you where it is."

Coogan thanked him. "Sounds like just the thing."

★ ★ ★

He woke once in the night to the sound of a horseman riding past in the street at a fair clip, and he wondered who could be setting out on a journey at that dark hour. But he did not give it much thought, and as the clip-clop of hoofs faded in the distance he fell asleep again.

2

COOGAN breakfasted with Lois Lloyd and half a dozen other persons who were making use of Mrs Goobey's lodging-house. Mrs Goobey herself was a widow, a lean starched-and-ironed no-nonsense sort of woman, but the accommodation merited Sheriff Loder's recommendation.

Somehow the word of what had occurred the previous day to the north of the town seemed to have got round, and Coogan caught a few interested glances cast at him. Only one man, however, who had the appearance of a travelling salesman, had the hardihood to make a direct reference to the subject.

"Hear you and the young lady had some trouble with a parcel of badmen out on the trail. That so?"

"Yep," Coogan said.

"Like to tell us about it?"

"Nope," Coogan said; and the look he gave the drummer discouraged him and anyone else from asking further questions regarding the incident.

After breakfast Coogan asked Lois what she intended doing about her father's travelling store, which presumably was still lying where it had come to rest and no doubt had some saleable merchandise inside it.

"What can I do?" she asked.

"You're not aiming to carry on the business on your own account."

She shook her head doubtfully. "I don't think that's a practical proposition."

Coogan was inclined to agree. "It's no occupation for a young woman on her own, that's for sure. So why don't you hire a buckboard and drive out there and bring the stuff into town? You could maybe make a sale of it."

She thought about the suggestion. Then she said: "Would you help me?"

It was not a job Coogan had been

looking for; he had other plans. But there was such an appealing look in her eyes, and he had to admit that she really was a fine-looking young female, not much more than twenty years old maybe, and maybe alone in the world now that her pa was gone . . . So what the hell! Was there anything else he could do but agree to lend her a hand?

"Okay," he said. "I'm just going to pay a call on the sheriff. After that we'll see what we can do."

Her eyes brightened and she gave a quick little smile, which was something he had not had from her until then and was worth waiting for.

"Thank you," she said. "Thank you, Brad."

Which was all fine and dandy, he thought, just so long as she was not getting any smart ideas in her head about tagging along with him when he left Pikeville. Because that was just not on the programme. Not on his programme anyway.

He found Deputy Mackley in the sheriff's office minding the store.

"Sheriff not in?"

Mackley looked all round the room. "Don't seem like it."

"Know where I can find him?"

"Guess not. When I came in this morning I found a note he'd left saying he had urgent business out of town and he'd be back later."

"And you don't know where this urgent business might have taken him?"

"The note didn't say. Your guess is as good as mine."

Coogan remembered the sound he had heard in the night of a horseman riding past Mrs Goobey's establishment. It could have been Loder. But what business would have come up to take him out of town at that hour?

"Does he often take off like that without telling you where he's going?"

"Naw; I wouldn't say often."

"Doesn't it surprise you?"

"Not that much. He's the sheriff. He don't have to answer to me for everything he does." Mackley gave Coogan a quizzing look. "Anything I can do for you?"

"I'd like to have a word with the prisoner, if that's permitted."

"It's okay by me," Mackley conceded, making no move to get up from his chair. "You know where he is. Help yourself."

Coogan found Krane lying on the bunk in his cell. He scowled at his visitor through the bars, apparently none too pleased to see him.

"What do you want?"

"A talk."

"We got nothin' to talk about."

"Sure, we have. Like where do I find Red Sheene?"

"Go to hell."

"I doubt whether he's got there yet. Give it time."

"Oh," Krane sneered, "ain't you the smart one! Well, mister, if you're really smart you'll stay clear of Red, 'cause after what you done yesterday he'll kill you, he surely will."

"Is that a fact? Well, maybe I'll kill him before he gets the chance. And maybe just for starters I'll kill you right here and now." Coogan drew his Colt forty-five from its holster and poked the barrel through the bars of the cell. "How about that?"

Krane sat up suddenly. "You wouldn't dare."

"Why not? I'd have killed you out there yesterday with the other two if I hadn't figured you might give me a lead to the boss man. But now I can see that you don't mean to do it, so I may as well kill you anyway. Save the hangman a job."

"You're bluffing," Krane said; but he sounded uncertain and looked more than a little apprehensive.

"Maybe I am and maybe I'm not. There's one sure way for you to find out. Just go on acting like a clam and I'll either shoot you or I won't." Coogan thumbed back the hammer of the Colt and took deliberate aim at Krane. "I'm going to count up to ten, and if you don't spill the beans by then you get a skinful of lead. Or you don't, as the case may be. It's up to you. You want to take the chance, okay; I'm not stopping you." He began to count slowly. "One, two — "

Krane licked his lips, staring at Coogan and the gun in his hand. "You wouldn't shoot me. You'd never get away with it. They'd hang you for sure."

Coogan just went on counting. He had reached seven when Krane's nerve failed and he began bawling for help, screaming bloody murder and retreating to the corner of the cell that was furthest away from the gun.

"Eight, nine," Coogan said. He stopped counting, eased the hammer of the Colt forward and slipped the weapon back into its holster just as the deputy sheriff appeared on the scene.

"What in hell's going on?" he demanded.

"That bastard was going to shoot me," Krane yelped. "He was going to kill me. Take his gun. Take it away from him."

Mackley's gaze shifted from Krane to Coogan. "What's eating him?"

Coogan shrugged. "Ah, he's crazy. He's got some bee in his bonnet. Don't give it a thought."

"Were you going to shoot him?"

"Now do I look that stupid? Shoot a man in here! With you just next door! That would really be asking for trouble, wouldn't it?"

Mackley looked at Krane. "You heard that?" Krane was calming down, shamefaced and sullen. "He threatened to kill me. He had his gun pointing at me and he said he'd plug me full of lead."

"And you believed him?"

"He meant it. He wasn't fooling. You ask him." Mackley turned to Coogan with a questioning lift of the eyebrows.

Coogan gave a thin icy smile. "It's like I said; the man's crazy."

"Maybe he is," Mackley said. "And

maybe he has reason to be. Well, you've had your talk with him and I guess you'd better go now before you make him even crazier."

"I'm on my way," Coogan said.

★ ★ ★

They hired a buckcart with a bony horse in the shafts from the livery stable on the edge of town which was owned by a man named Kurt Bergmann, a bluff chunky character who employed a stringy old black called Rastus as assistant. Coogan had left his own horse at Bergmann's for the night, and he let it stay there while he shared the seat on the buckcart with Miss Lloyd. He took the reins and they had to drive through the length of Pikeville before coming to the trail along which they had ridden to town the previous evening. There were more people on the street now, and several curious glances were turned on the pair on the buckcart.

"Looks like we're getting ourselves known around here," Coogan remarked. "You shoot a couple of badmen and people sit up and take notice."

"Does it bother you?"

"There's other things bother me more."

"Like what?"

"Never mind."

She was silent for a while after that as the buckcart rattled along the trail. Then she asked: "Where do you come from, Brad?"

"North of here. Wyoming way."

"You've had a long ride."

"Guess so."

"Tailing the Sheene gang?"

He glanced at her. He had not told her that. But of course she must have heard what he had said to Krane at that first meeting in the hollow.

"That's about it."

"Why?"

"There's a score to settle."

"Like to tell me about it?"

His immediate impulse was to refuse,

36

but then he changed his mind. Somehow or other there was that about her which invited confidence, and somewhat to his own surprise he found himself telling her.

"The Sheene gang killed my wife and daughter."

"Oh, Brad!" she said; and he felt her hand on his arm. "Oh, Brad!"

He told her how he had found them dead in the wreckage of the cabin, but he kept back the full horrific details of the crime; it was too grim a picture to paint for her, and he had no desire to dwell on it himself.

She said softly: "It makes two of us, doesn't it?"

"Two of us?"

"We both have a score to settle with Sheene."

She was of course referring to the death of her father. Sheene might not have been personally concerned in that; the three men who had done the deed had almost certainly not planned it beforehand but had come upon the travelling store quite by chance. Maybe they had attacked it more in a spirit of devilry than anything else; and there had been the girl to attract them. But they were Sheene's men and he could see why she would hold the gang leader ultimately responsible.

"We do, don't we, Brad?"

"Well, yes, I suppose you could say that."

"So why don't we join forces, you and me?"

It was what he had been afraid she had been leading up to. But it was out of the question.

"Now look," he said, "you know that's not possible."

"What's so impossible about it?"

"It's no job for a woman."

"Oh, I see," she said. "You think it's man's work and I wouldn't be able to handle it because I'm too weak. Well, let me tell you, Brad Coogan, I'm not weak. I can ride a horse and I can use a gun." She sounded angry, as though resenting the slur on her capabilities.

Coogan tried to placate her. "I'm sure you can. I'm sure you're strong and can do a whole raft of things. But all the same — "

"All the same you don't want me to ride with you?"

"Oh, it's not that I don't want you to."

"So what is it?"

"Well, it's just that I don't think it's a good idea."

He thought she was going to pursue the argument, but she seemed to have come to the conclusion that he would not change his mind, and she said no more on the subject. The rest of the journey was completed in a rather moody silence.

The wrecked wagon was just as they had left it the previous day; there appeared to have been no looting of the contents, and it was possible that no one had passed that way during the period of time that it had been lying there. But even if no human predators had been on the scene it was apparent that other kinds had been: the dead horse had been partly eaten, perhaps by coyotes and carrion-eaters of the winged variety; in fact some of these unlovely birds had retreated from the carcase at the approach of the buckcart, but they had not gone far and were still waiting around for another opportunity to enjoy the feast.

On one side the ground sloped gently down into the hollow and Coogan was able to drive the cart up close to the wreck. Without wasting further time he and Miss Lloyd began transferring goods from the wagon to the other vehicle. So engrossed were they in this task that they failed to observe the approach of a third person, and the first intimation they had of his presence was the sound of his voice.

"Hold it!"

They turned then and saw a man standing some twenty yards away from them. In his right hand he had a long-barrelled revolver. It was pointing at them.

Coogan's hand made an instinctive movement towards his own gun, but he froze when the man said sharply:

"Don't try it."

He was young, with clean-cut features and a debonair look about him. He was dressed all in black: hat, shirt, leather jacket, pants and boots. The only blemish on this sombre outfit was a sprinkling of dust which might have been acquired in the course of riding the trail. His horse was not in sight, but there could be little doubt that he had one, and Coogan guessed that the man had done what he himself had done the previous day: he had left the animal screened by the boulders and had approached silently to see what was going on in the hollow.

"What you doing?" he asked.

Coogan answered with some impatience. "You got eyes in your head. I guess you can see what. We're unloading the wagon and putting the hardware and such on the buckcart."

"Why?"

"You can see that too. The wagon's in no condition to travel. Likewise the horse; what's left of it."

"Your outfit?"

"No."

"Wouldn't be looting it, would you?"

"Hell, no. It belongs to the lady. I'm just lending a hand."

The newcomer glanced at Miss Lloyd. "That the truth, ma'am?"

"Of course it is. Do we look like thieves?"

He seemed to think about it for a few moments. Then he said: "Guess not."

"So why don't you put the shooter away," Coogan suggested. "Nobody's threatening you."

The young man gave a grin, lowered the revolver and stowed it in the holster on his belt. "So what happened?"

Coogan told him. The mention of the Sheene gang appeared to touch a nerve and he gave a low whistle.

"So this was their work! Well now!"

"You know about them?"

"I should. They killed my father. He

was a bank teller. They robbed the bank and shot him when he tried to stop the hellions."

"They killed my wife and daughter."

"Is that a fact!"

"And my father too," the girl said. "I'd say that makes us kind of a team, wouldn't you?"

"Now look," Coogan said, "I've told you — "

"What has he told you?" the man asked.

"That I can't ride with him on the trail of Sheene. Because I'm a woman."

"And you think that's no good reason?"

"Well, what do you think?"

"I'd have to give it some consideration. Might be advantages in the arrangement."

"Now let's get things straight," Coogan said. "I don't go for this team idea. I work on my own.

"When you're dealing with a villain like Butcher Sheene," the young man said, "it might be wise to use all the help you can get. And just so's we know who's who, my name's Matt Hanning."

Coogan, somewhat grudgingly, introduced himself and Lois Lloyd.

"You a bank teller too, Mr Hanning," Miss Lloyd asked.

The question seemed to amuse him. "Do I look like one?"

"Perhaps not."

"No. These little fellers are more in my line." He dipped a finger and thumb into one of his shirt pockets and fished out two playing-cards; one was a joker and the other was an ace of spades.

"You're a gambling man?"

"When I'm not engaged on other pursuits. Like tracking down my father's killers."

"And you make a living at it?"

"I get by."

"A tinhorn gambler!" Coogan spoke with some disgust. "That's just what we want."

Hanning refused to take offence. "Take it you don't go much on gamblers. Okay, let it pass. But I can ride as good as the next man and I can handle a gun a lot better than most."

Coogan looked at him doubtfully. "So?"

"So now I'll give you a hand with that gear, and then we can ride into town together."

Coogan thought the young fellow seemed to be taking a lot for granted, but it was difficult to raise any valid objection to what had been suggested, so he just gave a shrug and got on with the work. It was okay for Hanning to ride into town with them, but after that — well, they would see.

3

THE funeral took place early in the afternoon. The cemetery was situated on a piece of rising ground beyond the boundary of the town. It was a dreary place, with just one gaunt pine thrusting up from the ragged grass and the scattering of plain wooden crosses that marked the graves.

The coffins were all transported out to it on Zeke Nudd's buckboard, with Nudds and Mangin in attendance and two other hungry-looking individuals to help lower the bodies into the graves that had already been dug for them. At the cemetery the coffins were separated and Lloyd was interred at a respectable distance from the men who had caused his death.

Both Coogan and Matt Hanning joined the bereaved daughter in scattering a handful of earth on her father's coffin, the small stones making a hollow rattling sound as they fell on the rough wood. Coogan glanced at Lois to see how she was taking this last farewell, and he was relieved to see that she was perfectly calm; there were no tears, no public exhibition of emotion. Whatever grief she might be feeling, she was keeping it strictly under control, and he admired her for that.

On the way back into the town he asked her whether she needed any help in disposing of the goods salvaged from the wrecked wagon.

"Thank you," she said, "but I have already sold everything to the proprietor of the general store."

Coogan was surprised. "You didn't waste any time."

"Why should I? He offered me a fair price and I accepted. Maybe he got a bargain, but I wanted to be rid of the stuff and it was the easiest way."

"And what now?"

"How do you mean?"

"I mean what are your plans?"

"You haven't changed your mind?"

"In what way?" Coogan asked; though he knew the answer.

"You're still not willing to take me along with you?"

"I'm sorry," he said. And in a way he was, because in the short time he had known Miss Lloyd he had come to admire her more than a little, and if the circumstances had been different he might have been happy to have her company. And maybe not just for the present either. But as things were it was simply not possible. "It wouldn't work, you know."

"I think it would. But if you've made up your mind there's nothing I can do about it, is there? I'll just have to think of something else."

He was glad she had come to accept the situation and was not going to argue any more; he had a feeling that if she were to put any more pressure on him it might end up with his giving way to her persuasion. And that would have been all against his better judgement.

Hanning on the other hand was something altogether different. He wondered just how good with a gun the young fellow really was. Perhaps as a gambling man he needed to be good in order to stay alive.

★ ★ ★

Sheriff Loder was back in his office when the funeral party returned from burying the dead. Whatever business it was that had sent him riding off into the night had apparently been completed. Coogan paid another call on him and received a rather sour greeting. Loder looked worn out and grumpy.

"So you're still around."

"Yes, I'm still around. But not for much longer."

This information appeared to give the sheriff no pain. "Where you headin'?"

"South maybe."

Loder gave him a shrewd look.

"Wouldn't be hoping to get on the trail of the Sheene gang, would you?"

"What gives you that idea?" Coogan asked. He had said nothing to Loder about his quest.

"Just a thought. Luke tells me you been questioning the prisoner. Could be you was asking him where you could find Sheene."

"Why would I do that?"

"Maybe you got a grudge against him."

"Maybe I have."

"Take my advice," Loder said. "Forget it."

"Some things you just can't forget."

Loder shrugged. "Well, it's your funeral, I guess."

"I hope not," Coogan said. "I sure hope not."

* * *

Having quitted the sheriff's office Coogan went to settle up with Mrs Goobey and collect his belongings from

50

the lodging-house.

"So you're leaving already?" she said.

"Yes." Coogan thought he detected a note of regret in the widow's voice and he hoped it was not just because she was losing a paying guest. "I have to be on my way."

"Foot-loose and fancy-free. Well, if you're ever in this town again you know where to find a bed."

"And good food," Coogan said. "I'll remember."

He went next to get his horse from Bergmann's livery, where Rastus had done a good job of grooming on it. He paid the reckoning and added a tip for the groom which brought a wide grin to the black face.

"Thank you, Massa Coogan. And good luck to you."

As he led his horse out of the stable Coogan reflected that he might need all the luck that was going.

He rode out of town in the late afternoon without seeing a sign of Lois Lloyd. He had rather expected her to make one last effort to persuade him to let her go along with him, but whether deliberately or merely by chance, it seemed that she was keeping out of his way. Maybe she was sulking because of his refusal, but somehow she did not strike him as being the kind of girl who would do that. Anyway, whatever the reason, she was nowhere around to see him take his leave of Pikeville.

One person who did see him was Sheriff Loder, who was sitting on the porch at the front of his office with his feet up on the rail. He was smoking his corncob pipe, his sweat-stained hat pushed back from his forehead, and he gave a languid flip of the hand as Coogan rode past. Coogan thought the grin Loder gave as he waved farewell to the rider was a trifle sardonic, and he had an uneasy feeling that perhaps Loder knew something concerning his welfare that he himself did not. But perhaps that was just imagination.

He had been riding for maybe half an hour at an easy pace and was long out of sight of the town when he caught the sound of hoofbeats behind him. He reined in his horse and listened, and there could be no doubt that somebody was riding the trail which he had just covered. He could see no one because the trail hereabouts wound its way through a belt of trees and the view both behind and in front was restricted to a very short distance.

Coogan was wary. A horseman coming up behind at a pretty fair lick, as this one evidently was, could be perfectly harmless or could spell trouble. It was best to be prepared for any eventuality, and he dismounted, led his horse to one side under cover of the trees and eased the Winchester from its leather holder. Then he waited.

But not for long. He had scarcely settled himself when a rider came round a bend in the trail and into the view of the watcher in the trees. The horseman approached at a brisk canter, raising the dust, and in a few moments was level with the place where Coogan was hiding. He was gazing straight ahead and might have ridden past if Coogan had not given a shout.

"Whoa, there!"

Immediately the rider pulled his horse to a pebble-scattering halt and turned his head in the direction from which the shout had come. Coogan revealed himself, Winchester in hand.

"You in a hurry to get someplace?"

The man on the horse grinned. "Not now, I guess."

"Been following me, Matt?"

The man, who was indeed Hanning, gave a lift of the shoulders. "No sense denying it. You played a mean trick getting out of town without giving me the wink."

"Why should I do that?"

"I thought we had an understanding, Brad."

"What understanding would that be?"

"That I was to ride with you."

"Don't call to mind any understanding of that sort."

54

"Well, maybe it was more of a suggestion on my part. But I still reckon you could use a partner where you're heading. Waddya say?"

Coogan thought about it. It was true that he knew very little about Matt Hanning apart from the fact that he was a gambler, good-looking and a bit of a dandy; but he had reason to hate Sheene just as he, Coogan, had, and it might be worthwhile having him to lend a hand. Always supposing he was as good with a gun as he claimed he was.

"Why not give it a try?" Hanning urged. "What do you have to lose?"

Coogan came to a decision. "Okay, we'll do that. But just bear in mind you're only on probation. If things don't work out right we split. Understand?"

"Sure. I understand."

"Let's be on our way then. It'll be dark soon."

As they rode Coogan asked Hanning whether he had any knowledge of the whereabouts of the Sheene gang.

Hanning had to admit that he had no certain information on that point.

"But I did hear a rumour that they've got a hideaway in the San José Mountains."

"That could cover a pretty wide area."

"True. But we're heading that way and we could maybe pick up a clue someplace. Besides, the fact that some of the mob were operating just north of Pikeville makes it look like the rest might not be so far away. What you think?"

The same idea had occurred to Coogan. The San José Mountains had been visible from Pikeville and the foothills could not be far distant. It was the kind of country where a bunch like Sheene's vicious crew might well be holed up.

"I think you could be right," he said.

"Got any plans?"

"Nothing solid. Just taking things as they come."

"Well, let's hope for the best. Maybe Lady Luck will smile on us."

"Does she do that when you play cards?"

"Sometimes."

"You better pray to her then."

"I'll do that," Hanning said.

★ ★ ★

Darkness was falling when they decided to make camp for the night. It was at a place where a creek crossed the trail, flowing noisily over the pebbly shallows. They halted at the ford, dismounted and led the horses away to the left where large boulders and a few stunted trees provided a kind of natural shelter and a screen from anyone passing on the trail. Here they tethered the animals, unsaddled them and set about preparing a meal. It was a fine evening and a myriad stars glittered overhead in the cloudless sky. The air was fresh and cool.

When they had eaten they squatted

for a while by the fire of brushwood, smoking hand-rolled cigarettes and talking little, each busy with his own thoughts.

It was Hanning who heard the sound first. He had sharp hearing and he alerted Coogan.

"Someone's coming."

Then Coogan heard it, not loud, the kind of sound that might have been made by a person moving stealthily beyond the limits of the firelight. And anyone approaching in that manner could be up to no good. As if moved by the same impulse, the two men got to their feet and drew their guns. Coogan made a signal with his hand to indicate that Hanning should go to the left while he went to the right. Moving as stealthily as the intruder, they left the fire and skirted the boulders, one on one side and one on the other in order to carry out a pincer operation which would enclose the area from which the suspicious sound had come.

At first Coogan could make out

nothing but the dark shapes of the trees and he had to step carefully on the uneven ground. But careful though he was, his foot struck a loose fragment of rock and sent it rolling away. This sudden noise had an immediate and unforeseen effect. He heard a muffled exclamation such as anyone might utter involuntarily when startled, and a shadow moved no more than a few yards away from him.

"Stop!" Coogan snapped. "I've got you covered."

It was an exaggeration, but the words brought a swift reply, and this too was not at all what he might have expected.

"Oh, Brad, is that you?"

There was a note of relief in the voice, but this was not what struck Coogan as immediately as the fact that it was not a man's but a woman's; and hearing it he knew at once who it was who had been so stealthily approaching the campfire.

"Lois! What the devil are you doing here?"

She answered simply, as though it were too obvious really to need putting into words: "Looking for you, of course. What else would I be doing?"

"But how did you get here?" The thought came into his head that she might have walked from Pikeville, but he knew that this would have been impossible in the time.

"I rode," she said.

"Rode! But you don't have a horse."

"Oh, yes, I do. I left it back there." She made a vague gesture in the gloom. "When I saw your fire I tethered it and came on foot. I couldn't be sure it was you, so I had to be careful."

"You could have got yourself shot." Coogan stowed his gun away. "Where did you get the horse? You didn't have one when I left Pikeville."

"I bought it from Bergmann at the livery stable. With the money I got for my stock from the wagon."

Hanning appeared out of the shadows. He had heard the voices and had come to see what was going on.

"You can drop your gun, Matt," Coogan said. "Our night prowler is a lady."

Hanning came closer, peering at Lois.

"Hi, Matt!" she said.

"Well, I'll be damned! How did you get here?"

Coogan told him. "She's been following us. She bought herself a horse and got on our trail." He turned to the girl. "You just won't take no for an answer, will you?"

"Look," she said, "why don't you change your mind about me? I'd be a help; I promise."

"You'd just be in the way. Tell her, Matt."

But Hanning failed to give him wholehearted support. "Well, I don't know. Maybe we should talk it over some. Suppose we go back to the fire and have a chinwag. No sense hanging around here."

"Sounds like a good idea," Lois said. "I'll go get my horse."

61

She went off at once and Coogan turned on Hanning. "We're not taking her along and that's flat."

"Okay, so we're not taking her along." Hanning sounded cool. "It's your say so."

After a while Lois joined them by the campfire. They had heard her tethering her horse with theirs and she came into the firelight carrying her saddle and other gear, including a Winchester. It looked like a lot of weight for one so slightly built, but she was evidently stronger than she appeared to be because she seemed to be having no difficulty in managing the load.

"So you got yourself a gun too," Coogan said.

"Sure."

"Know how to use it?"

"I told you, didn't I? Anyway, would I buy one if I didn't? That would just be plain stupid."

"And you're expecting to need a gun?"

"If I'm going along with you I'd say that was more than likely."

"But you're not going with us. Didn't I make that clear to you?"

"Oh," she said, "you made it clear enough. But the way I look at it is this — how can you stop me? It's a free country, so I've been told."

Hanning gave a laugh and Coogan turned on him. "You think it's funny?"

"Sure. Don't you?"

"Damned if I do."

"Ah, don't make such a big thing of it. Leave it till morning. Let's all sleep on it."

Lois had dumped her gear on the opposite side of the fire from the two men. She was in her riding kit, a Stetson hat pushed to the back of her head, auburn hair visible beneath it. With the firelight playing on her face she looked young and attractive. Coogan had to admit as much to himself, and he wondered whether he really wanted to be rid of her. In different circumstances she might have

63

been real nice to have around.

"You like some coffee, Lois?" Hanning asked.

She accepted the offer, hunkered down and began to drink from the tin mug.

"Now," Hanning said, "this is what I call mighty cosy. Sure do."

Coogan gave a snort.

Hanning grinned at the girl. "Don't mind him. He's just feeling grouchy. He'll get over it."

"Oh, I'm sure he will," she said. "And I don't mind at all."

"Well now," Coogan said, "that is nice to know. Now we can all sleep happy."

Hanning grinned again. "See what I mean? Grouchy."

The girl just smiled. She seemed happy enough with the way things were going.

4

COOGAN woke suddenly to the pounding of horses' hoofs. He sat up, immediately on the alert. The moon had risen and was bathing everything in its silvery light. the fire had died down to glowing embers.

Coogan got up and walked quickly to the boulders that stood between the campfire and the trail, carrying his rifle with him. From a vantage point he was able to get a view of the ford glittering in the moonlight where the water rippled over the pebbly shallows. The sound of hoofs drumming on the ground had become louder and a moment later the horsemen came into sight, a number of them, some in long white coats, all silent and riding hard. They scarcely checked at all as they came to the ford, but went splashing through and out the other side.

They passed not more than twenty yards from where Coogan was standing and did not glance in his direction. It was impossible to see their faces clearly, but there was something oddly sinister about that closely bunched group riding as though with some fixed purpose in mind, with a giant of a man on a big grey horse in the lead. Then they had gone, disappearing down the trail in the direction of Pikeville.

"Who were they, Brad?"

It was Lois's voice and it startled him. He had not heard her approach, but now she was standing beside him. Evidently she also had been awakened by the passing band of horsemen.

"I don't know," he said. "All I know was they were going someplace in a hurry."

"Pikeville?"

"That's the way they were heading."

"What would they be going there for at this time of night?"

"Who knows?" Coogan said. But

he was reflecting that a bunch like that would surely not be riding hell for leather through the night on any benevolent mission. There had been a smell of evil about them; a smell he did not like.

Lois shivered. "I think they were badmen."

"You could be right at that," Coogan said. He had not cared for the look of them at all. But there was nothing to be done about it. "Let's go back and get some sleep."

Later he heard the pounding hoofs again, and he was quickly at the vantage point from which he had watched the horsemen go by earlier. Now he saw them returning, the giant on the big grey leading as before. The moon was lower in the sky and he could not see them so clearly; they were not riding quite so fast, but they were still bunched together and he saw them come to the ford and go splashing through. A few moments later they had disappeared into the night. The sound of hoofs was audible for a while longer, then it faded and died away into silence.

Lois had been awakened again and was again by his side. "So they came back."

"Yes, they came back."

He felt her hand on his arm. "That big man in the lead; did you see him?"

"Yes."

"What a monster he looked on that big grey horse."

It was apparent that she had been impressed by the leader of the cavalcade and that the impression had not been a pleasant one. She sounded subdued, and Coogan had a feeling that she might have touched his arm in a kind of instinctive gesture of comradeship, perhaps to draw courage from the contact. There could be no doubt that that dark giant of a horseman had been enough to strike fear to any heart. He did his best to reassure her.

"Don't let it bother you. He was only a man."

"I know. And yet I had this odd thought that if it had been the Devil on horseback he might have looked like that."

Coogan gave a laugh. "Now you're letting your imagination run away with you. Believe me, if he was a devil he was a very human one. There are plenty of those."

"Yes, of course. You have to be right. But maybe at that the human devils are the worst of the lot."

She turned and walked away, and Coogan sensed that he had offended her, perhaps with his laughter. He regretted it now, because really there had been nothing to laugh at and it had broken that sense of intimacy between them which had been engendered by the touch on his arm.

He followed her back to the fire and saw that Hanning was still asleep. The younger man had not been awakened either time by the horsemen riding past. He remarked on it to the girl.

"Our friend Matt is a sound sleeper."

"So it seems. Does it matter?"

"Not tonight. But there are times when it pays to sleep with one eye open."

"That's true."

Coogan put more wood on the embers of the fire to keep it going and wrapped himself again in his blanket, the saddle acting as a pillow. The next time he awoke he discovered that it was daylight and there was a pleasing odour of fresh-brewed coffee and frying bacon. Lois was by the fire preparing breakfast and she turned her head as she heard him stirring. She spoke with a touch of mockery.

"I wondered when you were going to wake up. Who was it talked about sleeping with one eye open?"

Coogan pushed fingers through his hair and got to his feet. "One up to you, Lois. You don't make much noise."

Hanning was still sleeping. Coogan roused him with a toe in the ribs and he got up yawning.

"My!" he said, "That's a lovely smell. Don't know about you, Brad, but I'd say the lady has her uses. We could do worse than take her along if only to handle the chores."

Coogan said nothing. He had come to the conclusion that it was useless to make any further objections; if Miss Lloyd had made up her mind to tag along there was not much he could do about it and he might as well accept the situation.

Lois said: "We've got news for you, Matt. There were people around during the night."

"People! What are you talking about?"

She told him about the horsemen.

"And you think they were up to no good?"

"At that time of night!" Coogan said. "What do you think?"

"Could they have been some of Sheene's bunch?"

It was a possibility that had already occurred to Coogan. "I'd say it's more than possible."

"You should've waked me. We could have given the bastards a dose of lead."

"Without knowing for certain who they were? That would've been plumb crazy."

"I guess you're right," Hanning admitted.

"You bet I'm right."

"There's one thing though. If they were Sheene's lot it shows they must be holed up not far away."

"I thought we'd already come to that conclusion."

"Well, it confirms it."

"If it was them."

* * *

As soon as they had breakfasted they hit the trail again. On the other side of the ford they picked up the traces of the party of horsemen who had ridden by in the night; the hoof-marks were easy to follow and it appeared that no one had passed that way since they had been made.

"This is a break for us," Hanning said. "It could lead us right to the place we're looking for."

Coogan was less optimistic. "Maybe. But it's my experience that things never work out as easy as that."

Nevertheless, the traces left by the nocturnal party continued to be plainly marked and remained on the trail for about a mile, after which they broke away to the left and went on in the general direction of the San José Mountains. Between these and the trail was open rolling grassland and the prints of the horses were still visible enough to follow.

"Looks like we were right," Hanning remarked. "They have got a hideout in the mountains."

Coogan had to agree. "But once we leave the grass it won't be so easy to find their tracks; the ground will be rocky."

He was thinking too that they had no plan of action worked out if they did find the gang's lair. A frontal assault by two men and a girl was hardly likely to be successful against the numbers of hard-bitten desperadoes that Red Sheene had gathered around him. Still, it had not come to that yet.

And in fact it never was to come to it; for a little later they reached a place where the hoof-marks of the horses became less discernible, and to make matters worse the prints seemed to be mixed in with those of some cattle that had recently been grazing there.

Coogan called a halt and gazed into the distance ahead. He could see the nearest of the mountains, a long razor-backed ridge of no great altitude with higher peaks visible behind it, snow-capped and majestic.

"Now what?" Hanning asked.

"I guess we'll just have to continue the way we've been going and hope to pick up the scent again farther on."

"Guess you're right."

Then Lois said softly: "Oh, oh, we've got company."

Coogan turned his head and saw

what she meant. A group of horsemen had appeared on the right. Until this moment they had been hidden from view on the far side of rising ground, but now they were on the brow of the rise and it was obvious that they had seen the other three halted on the lower level. There were ten of them, and after a brief hesitation they began to approach at a brisk trot.

"Now," Hanning said, "the question is do we stay or do we run?"

"Why should we run?" Coogan asked.

"Suppose those boys are the lot we've been trailing?"

"Is it likely? Our bunch passed by here hours ago and they were heading in a different direction."

By this time the ten had halved the distance between themselves and the three. Coogan, Hannay and Lois remained in their saddles, waiting.

"Looks like a handful of cowboys to me," Coogan said.

The other party came to a halt a few

yards short of the smaller group.

"Howdy, fellers!" Coogan said, keeping it friendly.

The friendliness was not echoed by the apparent leader of the ten. He was a lean tough-looking individual, maybe forty years of age, with a long bony face burned by the sun to the colour of old mahogany.

"Where you guys from?" he asked.

It was Coogan who answered. "Pikeville."

"Pikeville, huh? That your home town?"

"Can't say it is. Just passing through."

"Where you heading?"

"Where the trail takes us."

"You ain't on no trail. This here is the Circle Q ranch, Mr De Quincey's land. My name's Devon. I'm the ranch foreman. What's your name?"

Coogan told him. He also introduced Hanning and Miss Lloyd.

Devon stared at him suspiciously. The other men looked on in silence, grim-faced. There seemed to be an atmosphere of suspicion all round.

Finally Devon said: "I guess you better come with us."

"Where to?"

"The ranch-house."

"Why should we go there?"

"Mr De Quincey will want to talk to you, I guess."

"Now that," Coogan said, "sounds mighty improbable to me. Until this moment I'd never heard of the man. Why would he want to talk to any of us?"

"You'll see."

"Suppose we don't want to talk to him? Suppose we just want to go on our way?"

Devon's voice hardened. "Don't make trouble. Hell, there's enough of that around already. You comm' easy or does it have to be the hard way?"

Hanning's right hand dropped to the butt of his revolver. "Now look — "

"Don't try it, son," Devon said. He sounded tired. "There's ten of us.

That's more than three to one. Be sensible."

"He's right, Matt," Coogan said. "Better do as the man says."

Hanning seemed prepared to argue the point, but Coogan gave him a hard look and he decided not to. "Okay, let's go have a talk with this Mr De Quincey. Maybe we'll learn something."

"Now you're being sensible," Devon said. "Let's go."

* * *

It was an hour's ride. They travelled southward with the mountains always visible in the distance to the east. Cattle with the Circle Q brand roamed at will over this vast acreage of grass, their numbers giving some indication of the wealth of their owner.

The ranch-house, when they came to it, strengthened this impression; it was large and imposing, built partly of stone and partly of timber, a far cry from the crude log cabin in which Coogan had lived with his wife and child before the coming of the Sheene gang. At a respectable distance from it were other buildings: a vast barn, bunkhouse for the cowhands, stabling, sheds for various purposes, a smithy . . . In a corral were some fine-looking horses. Shade trees were growing here and there to add to the attractiveness of the layout, and all in all it was the kind of property that any man might have been proud to call his own.

Devon pointed out a hitching-rail where Coogan and his two companions could tether their horses.

"Wait there," he said, "while I go and have a word with Mr De Quincey. I'll give you a shout if he's ready to see you."

"My!" Hanning remarked. "We do feel honoured."

Devon ignored the sarcasm and walked away. They watched him mount the steps to the portico at the front of the house and go inside. Five minutes later he appeared again and beckoned to them.

"Looks like the boss man is ready to spare us a moment of his valuable time," Hanning said. "Better go."

They joined Devon on the portico and he led the way to a spacious room with a scattering of rich-looking rugs on the polished wood floor. It was equipped with some good solid furniture and there were brass lamps hanging from the ceiling and on the walls a number of framed oil paintings of scenes on the range. In a wide open fireplace some logs were burning and above the mantel-piece hung two flintlock muskets and a pair of muzzle-loading pistols. Standing with his back to the fire was a man who hardly needed to introduce himself as De Quincey.

There was an aristocratic look about him. He was tall and slim, his lean hawklike face embellished with a neatly trimmed moustache. His hair was silvery white but there was still an abundance of it though he was no longer young, and his eyes under the bushy brows had a keen piercing quality, as if they were capable of revealing to him the inner working of a man's brain.

"Ah!" he said. "Our visitors!"

He was elegantly dressed in cord breeches and polished riding-boots, a check waistcoat and a long tweed jacket. His silk cravat was adorned with a gold pin in which a diamond sparkled.

"Not visitors by choice," Coogan said. "We had a pressing invitation which was hard to refuse."

"I apologise for that. My foreman was perhaps a shade too zealous. But you were on my land."

"Is that a crime?"

"In itself, no. However, the circumstances are rather out of the ordinary."

"In what way?"

"One of my men has recently been killed. He was out on the range. His horse came back riderless. A search party found his body. He had been shot."

Coogan stared at him. "And you think we had something to do with that?"

De Quincey shook his head. "Frankly, no. But my men are suspicious of all strangers. Rightly so, I think."

"Do you have any idea who did the killing?"

"Oh, yes. It was almost certainly carried out by a bunch of outlaws we've been having trouble with for some time."

"You wouldn't be talking about the Sheene gang, would you?"

De Quincey looked surprised. "Why, yes. So you know about them?"

"I have good reason to. So have Matt Hanning here and Miss Lloyd. We've all had people very dear to us murdered by those swine."

"I see. And would that be the reason why you are in these parts?"

"Yes."

"Now let's get this straight," De

Quincey said. "Are you telling me that you've been following the Sheene gang? Searching for them, in fact?"

"That's about the size of it."

"And if you find them, what then?"

"Then we do what we have to do."

"By that I assume you mean you'll take vengeance on Butcher Sheene and his crew?"

"That's so."

"Two men and a woman! Do you have any idea of what you're taking on?"

"Yes."

"And yet you mean to press on with it?"

"We do."

Devon gave a derisive laugh. "You'll get yourselves killed. That's if you ever get near Sheene."

"Maybe so. Maybe not so. And for your information perhaps I should tell you that two of the gang are already in the Pikeville burying ground and one is behind bars in the sheriffs office. I'd

83

call that quite a fair start, wouldn't you?"

Devon looked disbelieving. "Are you telling us you three put them there?"

"No," Hanning said. "He did that on his own. It was before I made his acquaintance. Let me tell you this Mr Coogan is a pretty tough cookie."

"As a matter of interest," Coogan said, "the dead men were named Art Waters and Joe Bradley. The one inside bars is Ben Krane. He got a slug in the arm but he'll live. Perhaps he'll even live long enough to give the hangman a job."

Devon said nothing, but he was looking at Coogan with a deal more respect than he had shown hitherto.

De Quincey said: "I'll be interested to hear more."

"Some other time," Coogan said. "Right now if you have no objection we'll be on our way."

"Hunting the Sheene gang?"

"That's what we came this way for."

"Where do you hope to find them?"

"We heard a rumour they've got a hideout in the San José Mountains."

"And that's where you propose to go looking for it?"

"Sure."

De Quincey gave a wry smile. "Suppose I tell you I've had men searching for that hideaway for years without a trace of success. There's been lawmen too, but they couldn't find it either. What makes you think you'll do any better?"

"Maybe we'll strike lucky."

"Maybe you will at that. Beginner's luck. But I'm going to make a suggestion. Since we're all concerned with the same object, why don't you make this your base for operations? There's plenty of spare accommodation here and you're welcome to it for as long as you like. What do you say?"

Coogan glanced at Hanning and Lois, inviting their opinion, and it was the girl who answered.

"That's very generous of you, Mr De Quincey. And of course we'll be delighted to take advantage of the offer, won't we, Brad?"

Coogan shrugged. "If that's the way you feel. How about you, Matt?"

"Suits me," Hanning said.

5

THEY decided to go back to the place where they had been intercepted by the Circle Q party and try to pick up from there the trail of the men they now felt certain were members of the Sheene gang. But they were unsuccessful and they could think of no better course of action than to ride towards the mountains and make a search for anything that might look at all like a possible entrance to the outlaws' hideaway.

But they found nothing. Stretching away to the north and the south the ridge they had seen from the distance appeared to present an unbroken barrier, sloping reasonably gently to a certain height but then becoming so steep that it resembled nothing so much as an unbroken wall of rock which even an experienced mountaineer might have had great difficulty in scaling. Nowhere did there appear to be any place where a horse or a man could have progressed beyond the lower slopes.

"Yet they must have come this way," Hanning said. "So where did they go? Have they found the secret of vanishing into thin air?"

"I've never come across a man or a horse that could do a vanishing trick." Coogan sounded out of temper; it had been a frustrating day, and now evening was closing in with nothing accomplished. "They must be around here someplace."

"Sure they must. But we're not going to find them. Not today."

"Matt's right," Lois said. "I think we should go back to the ranch-house and try again tomorrow. You know what Mr De Quincey said: his men and others have been looking for Sheene's lair a long time and nobody's found it yet, so it must be well hidden. It wasn't likely that we'd drop on it straightaway."

Reluctantly Coogan had to admit that there was truth in this; and though he hated giving up the search even temporarily he knew that no good purpose would be served by stumbling around in failing light.

"Okay. Let's call it a day."

It was dark by the time they reached the ranch buildings; for the last part of the way they had in fact been guided by the lights showing around the place. De Quincey seemed pleased to see them.

"I was beginning to think you were not coming back. Did you have any luck?"

Coogan shook his head. "None."

De Quincey did not say he had expected nothing better, but it was pretty obvious that he had not. "They're a cunning bunch and they'll take some catching. But some day, some day, by God, Butcher Sheene is going to get his come-uppance."

"It can't be too soon," Coogan said.

Later De Quincey volunteered some information about himself. Coogan guessed that he was glad to have somebody to talk to besides his foreman. He was a widower and apparently led a rather lonely life in the big house where he was looked after by a middle-aged manservant named Henry Makins and his wife Sarah who did the cooking.

Ralph De Quincey was not one of those wealthy ranchers who had clawed their way up from nothing; he had been born the younger son of an English squire and had early conceived a passion for the American West. He had persuaded his father to let him learn the cattle-raising business on the ranch of a successful American cattleman with whom the senior De Quincey was acquainted, and at the age of twenty-three he had acquired some land and stock of his own with money provided by his father. He must have been one of those fortunate beings who know what they want to do and do it well; he had apparently prospered from the start. He had married an American girl and it had been a very happy partnership, which was destined to come to a tragic end when Mrs De Quincey was thrown from a horse and died from the injuries she received.

There was one child, a daughter named Marian. She was now twenty-one and had been staying with some relations of her mother's in New York for the past three months. But now she was on her way back to the Circle Q and was in fact expected to arrive the next day. Henry Makins would be meeting her at the staging post with the buggy.

When he spoke of his daughter De Quincey's normally stern features appeared to soften, and it was obvious to Coogan that she meant a great deal to him.

"You will be glad to have her back home with you, Mr De Quincey."

"Indeed I shall. Place is not the same without her. If anything were to happen to her — But there, why should it?"

Yes, Coogan thought, why should it? But he had had a daughter and something had happened to her, something horrible in the extreme. Merely thinking of it now was enough to rouse the anger in him, the hatred of Sheene and all his gang. But he would get the man yet.

He and his two companions set off early in the morning to resume their search. Late in the afternoon they returned, having had no more success than on the previous day. They were all feeling weary and depressed, but they had not given up hope.

They had been expecting to find Marian De Quincey returned home to the delight of her father, but they found a house almost in a state of mourning and De Quincey himself in a mood verging on despair.

His daughter, the apple of his eye, had been kidnapped.

At first he seemed disinclined to speak about it, as though recounting events to them would be too painful for him to bear. But gradually the story came out, and they could well understand how shattered he was, how possessed by this mixture of anguish, loss and impotent rage.

For the man into whose hands Marian had fallen was none other than that evil monster, Butcher Sheene.

It was Henry Makins who had brought the news. He had set off in mid-morning to drive the buggy to the staging post some ten miles distant, there to pick up Miss De Quincey with her baggage. According to his account he had arrived in good time at the rendezvous only to find the place occupied by Sheene and his men, with Jeremiah Hicks, the keeper of the post, and his wife lying dead in one of the rooms, covered in blood from gunshot wounds.

Makins was seized as soon as he drove up and was questioned by the outlaws. Without thinking he told them he had come to collect the daughter of Rancher De Quincey from the stagecoach and take her back to the Circle Q ranch. Nothing could have delighted Sheene more than this information. It appeared that his gang had taken over the post with the object of robbing the stage as soon as it rolled in; but now he saw a way of making a great deal more profit from the raid.

So Makins had been forced to wait out of sight until the stage arrived. The outlaws had also been hidden away until it pulled to a halt, but then they rushed out with guns in their hands. The guard was foolish enough to reach for his shotgun and got himself a chestful of lead for his pains, which effectively eliminated him from the reckoning.

The driver, a leathery little man named Jack Wells, promptly reached for the sky and froze. He was ordered to come down from his seat, which he did pronto. The stage was carrying six passengers inside and two outside, both men. Of the insides only two were female; Miss De Quincey and a plump middle-aged woman with a painted face and flashy clothes who might well have been the madam of a whorehouse.

Sheene ordered two of his men to remove the girl and take care of her. Then the rest of the gang began relieving the other passengers of everything they were carrying of any value. When this task was completed Sheene personally carried out the kind of bloody operation that had earned him his sobriquet of Butcher. He cut the passengers' throats with a hunting-knife.

Makins was a horrified witness of this barbarity, and he heard the screaming and the plaintive cries for mercy which went unheeded by the ruffians. He said that some of the victims tried to get away, but Sheene's men grabbed them and held them while their leader got busy with the knife. It was a sight, he said, that would haunt him for the rest of his life.

By this time the coach was running with blood, and the two outside passengers were stowed inside with the other bodies. Then Sheene ordered Jack Wells to get back on the box and drive on. Wells, no doubt only too thankful to be alive, needed no urging, and the stage with its gruesome cargo rolled away down the trail, heading for the town of Garfield which was the next scheduled halt on the route.

Makins was now in considerable fear for his own life, but in fact he was in no danger because Sheene had a use for him; he was to be the messenger who would carry the news to De Quincey that his daughter had been kidnapped and was being held to ransom. Makins was reluctant to leave the terrified girl in such rough hands, but he had no alternative; so he returned with the buggy and a demand for twenty thousand dollars to be paid in exchange for her freedom.

Coogan gave a low whistle when De Quincey mentioned the amount of the ransom demand. "That's a lot of money."

De Quincey made a dismissive

gesture. "It's nothing compared to my daughter's safety."

"So you'll pay?"

"Of course I'll pay. What else can I do? I shall drive into Garfield tomorrow and draw the cash from the bank."

Sheene had given De Quincey two days to come up with the dollars, probably figuring that he would need time to raise such a large sum. Then one man was to bring the money at noon to a rendezvous at a place called Black Rock. If more than one man came the deal was off and Sheene would not answer for Miss De Quincey's safety. This thinly-veiled threat coming from a man like Sheene was enough to make the blood run cold in the veins of anyone interested in her welfare, and Coogan could understand why De Quincey would not hesitate to pay the ransom.

"Who will you send with the money?"

"I haven't decided yet."

"Let me take it," Coogan said.

"You!"

"Oh, I know what you're thinking. How can you trust a man you'd never set eyes on before yesterday? What's to prevent me from just riding off with the money?"

"And what would be your answer to such questions?"

"Just that I'm interested in only one thing: bringing Sheene to book. Your money doesn't mean a thing to me; all I want is that man and his gang."

"And how would this help you in that respect?"

"I don't know. But I reckon I might pick up some clue to his hideaway; don't you think it's just a possibility? Anyway, it would do no harm for me to act as the go-between. If you trust me."

De Quincey gave him a long hard look. Then he said: "I'll think about it."

There was no more to be done that day, but before De Quincey set off the next morning a posse of armed men rode up to the ranch-house under the command of Sheriff Van Doren of Garfield. The arrival in town the previous day of the stagecoach with its slaughtered passengers had produced a sensation of horror and revulsion among the inhabitants. Van Doren had at once set about collecting a posse to hunt for the perpetrators of the outrage, but by the time he had got the party organised it was growing dark and was too late to set out on the chase. Instead, they had started at dawn the following morning and were at the De Quincey place very early in the day.

Van Doren consulted with De Quincey and was told about the kidnap and ransom demand. He looked grave when he heard this and sucked his teeth.

"You're going to pay up?"

"I have no choice."

Van Doren was a broad-shouldered man with a craggy face and pale blue eyes. Coogan thought he looked a deal more trustworthy than Loder, the

Pikeville sheriff. Lawmen came in all shapes and sizes.

"A man like that," Van Doren said, "could be planning a double-cross. It'd be in his nature."

"It's a risk I have to take."

"Guess you do at that."

After his talk with De Quincey Van Doren took off with his posse to scour the land for any sign of the Sheene gang. He called at the ranch-house on his way back later in the day to report a complete lack of success. Not for the first time Butcher Sheene and his men had done the disappearing act.

"Not hide nor hair of them," Van Doren said disgustedly. "Vanished like a wisp of smoke. How do they do it?"

"I wish I knew," De Quincey said. "I just wish I knew. But it's a mystery."

During the day he himself had made a journey to the bank in Garfield to draw out the twenty thousand dollars. He had travelled in the buggy with Makins driving and an escort of well-armed cowhands. He was taking no

100

risks with that kind of money in his possession.

Meanwhile, following directions given by Devon, Coogan rode out to the rendezvous named by Sheene. Black Rock was an easily identified landmark, since there was nothing else at all like it anywhere around. It was like an old rotten tooth of gigantic size thrusting up from the ground to a height of more than a hundred feet, the sides steep and with scarcely a toe hold for any climber who might have been intrepid enough to attempt to scale them.

"So," Hanning said, "this is the place of assignation."

He and Lois had accompanied Coogan on the reconnaissance, and now the three of them walked their horses round the outcrop and gazed towards the mountains from which direction Sheene's emissary would almost certainly come on the morrow, bringing the girl with him to exchange for the ransom money.

It was a suitable spot for such a transaction, commanding as it did a clear view all round for a distance of up to a mile. No one could fall into an ambush there.

"I don't like it," Lois said. She looked at Coogan with some concern. "If Mr De Quincey accepts your offer I think you could be walking into a trap."

"I doubt it," Coogan replied. "It'll just be a straightforward exchange. I hand over the money and bring the young lady home."

"Things seldom go according to plan."

Coogan grinned at her. "You worry too much, Lois." But he knew she was right.

Back at the ranch-house he asked De Quincey whether he had come to any decision regarding whom he was going to send to Black Rock with the ransom money. The rancher had apparently given some careful thought to the matter on the journey to and from the Garfield bank and had made his choice of courier.

"I'm going to trust you, Coogan."

"I'm glad," Coogan said. "I promise you won't have any reason to regret it."

"I hope not. I certainly hope not."

Later that evening as he was leaning on the rail of the corral, smoking a cigarette and thinking, he was joined by Lois.

"I've been looking for you," she said.

"What's on your mind?"

"Have you talked to Mr De Quincey."

"Yes."

"Well? Is he sending you?"

"He is."

He could not see her expression in the gloom but her words told him that she was not overjoyed. "I wish he'd decided to send somebody else."

"Why?"

"Oh, I don't know. It's just this feeling I have that something will go wrong."

"Forget it. Nothing's going to go wrong."

"It's easy to say that. But how can you be sure?"

"I can't," he admitted. "No one can ever be entirely certain how things will turn out. It's a chance we all have to take."

"Ah, so you agree there is some risk?"

"I didn't say that."

"But it's what you meant."

"And if it was? There's risk in everything. When you get on a horse you risk being thrown and breaking your neck. Life is full of risks. We have to accept the fact."

"It's not the same. I wish you weren't going. You didn't have to take the job; any one of De Quincey's men would have done it."

"I guess they would. But I want to do it. And frankly I don't see why you're so bothered. Even if there is a risk I'm the one that's taking it. What's it to you?"

The question seemed to goad her into a fit of sudden exasperation. "Oh, damn you, Brad! Don't you understand? Don't you really understand? I love you. God knows why, but I love you."

He was taken completely out of his stride; so much so that for a moment he was lost for words and did not move. And when he did it was too late because she had turned abruptly away from him and was running towards the lighted portico. He thought of following her, but before he could make up his mind to do so she had gone inside and he was left to ponder on what she had said and wonder whether to feel elated or depressed.

It was too soon, of course. Coming so quickly after the tragedy back home in Wyoming it was all too soon. But the hard fact was that life had to go on and a man could not mourn the dead for ever. There would come a time after this present business was finished, a future he had so far avoided contemplating. But he would have to face up to it eventually — if he lived. And then?

And then perhaps . . . Who could tell?

6

HE set out for the rendezvous at Black Rock with the money in the saddle-bags and leading a spare horse for Marian De Quincey to ride, since it seemed unlikely that Sheene would allow her to complete the journey home on one of his.

He had allowed himself plenty of time to reach his destination well before noon without forcing the pace, and it was a fine sunny day with only a few thin wisps of cloud in the sky. He hoped this was a good omen but he did not put much faith in it; good or bad, the weather was immaterial.

He had spoken scarcely a word to Lois that morning, and he had the impression that she was avoiding him. Possibly she was feeling rather diffident after that outburst of the previous evening; maybe she even regretted having made such a revelation regarding the state of her feeling for him. Whatever the reason, she had given him no opportunity to broach the subject to her; and in a way he was not sorry, since it was hardly the time to talk about such matters. Better to wait until the present business was concluded.

He came to the rock half an hour before noon, and he could see no one. He dismounted and rolled a cigarette and lit it and waited. The sun was hot as it came up to the zenith and there was little shade from the rock; the San José Mountains shimmered in the distance and he wondered just where in that massive range the Sheene gang had its lair. There were many people who would have given much for that secret, many who had suffered at the cruel hands of the bloodthirsty desperadoes.

He had smoked half the cigarette when he discerned something moving a long way off in the direction of the foothills. He kept his eyes on the object and saw it gradually resolve itself into the shape of two horse-riders coming towards him. He had little doubt that these two were Miss De Quincey and the outlaw who had been deputed to escort her to the rock and collect the ransom money.

So far, so good. All appeared to be going according to plan.

It was not until some time later that he began to suspect that something was wrong. The riders had now become more clearly seen as they drew closer to the place where he was waiting for them, and it seemed to him that neither of them had the appearance of a woman. He could not be certain yet, but before long there could be no doubt that the riders were both men.

It was obvious now that the business was not going as he and De Quincey had expected, although this might have been Sheene's intention all along. He had not precisely said that the girl would be brought to Black Rock, only that the rendezvous was to be made there. Coogan did a bit of rapid thinking and decided to do some parleying when the men arrived; and it seemed to him that he would be in a better position to parley if he was at the butt-end of a gun.

So he took the Winchester in his hands and stood with the horse concealing the weapon from the approaching riders. They came on at an easy pace, and soon he could see that one of them appeared to be a Mexican; he was fat and swarthy and he was wearing flared pants and a short jacket and a wide-brimmed sombrero. He had a black drooping moustache and a bandolier of cartridges slung over his left shoulder. He looked like a brigand.

The other man, though no less villainous in appearance, was certainly no Mexican; he was hollow-chested and stringy, dressed in a sweat-stained blue shirt, well-worn blue pants and a peaked army cap. He had a long chin, a prominent nose and squinting eyes.

His skin was deeply tanned and the lower part of his face was covered by a dark stubble.

When these two had approached to within ten yards of him Coogan brought the Winchester into view and pointed it at them.

"Stop there!"

They reined in their horses and looked at him. They seemed surprised but unconcerned. Then the one in the army cap said in a nasal drawl:

"What's this, feller? You know what we're here for, so why the gun?"

"Looks to me like you forgot something."

"Now what would that be?"

"The lady."

They both laughed.

"What's so funny?" Coogan asked. "Tell me the joke and let me have a laugh too."

"The joke is you thinking we was going to bring her with us. That's real hilarious, ain't it, Mex?"

The Mexican just grinned, revealing

tobacco-stained teeth.

"I don't see the joke," Coogan said. "The way I heard it you were to bring Miss De Quincey and I was to bring the money. Then we were to make the exchange."

The man in the army cap shook his head. "You heard wrong. What's your name, feller?"

"Brad," Coogan said, omitting the surname.

"I'm Roper. This here is Mex. Now we all know each other. That's nice, huh?"

"I still don't know why you didn't bring Miss De Quincey."

"Well, figure it out," Roper said. "Suppose we'd brought her and there'd been men waiting someplace like the other side that rock maybe; jest waiting to pounce on us soon's we got there. That way you'd have the lady and you'd keep the dollars, and Mex and me, we'd be in bad trouble, wouldn't we?"

"There's no one hiding."

"Well, maybe there ain't. But how was we to know? We don't take nothin' for granted. Safer if we take you back with us and you bring the lady out when you've delivered the cash. You got it, ain't you?"

"Yes, I have."

"Let's see. Put the gun away. You don't need it. Nobody's going to start shootin'."

Coogan thought about it. It was obvious that if he went with the men he would be putting his head into a noose, because there was no guarantee that Sheene would let him go again, taking the kidnapped girl with him. There would be nothing to prevent the gang leader from keeping the money and the hostage and putting a bullet in his, Coogan's, brain for good measure.

Yet if he called the whole thing off now and rode back to the ranch-house with the dollars and no girl what sort of a man would he appear to be in De Quincey's eyes? And in Lois's? Somebody who was too yellow to risk his own skin? Oh, sure, he might argue that no prudent person would carry the ransom money right into the kidnappers' den when there was no guarantee that he would ever come out again; but would anybody listen? Would he not simply be branded as a coward?

And besides, was not this the opportunity he had been looking for? Here was the chance to discover the outlaws' lair; so was he going to throw it away because of a whiff of danger? When you went hunting a man like Sheene you had to accept danger as one of the hazards. And he wanted Sheene, wanted him real bad.

He lowered the Winchester and stowed it away.

"That's the boy," Roper said. "Now show us the cash."

Coogan opened one of the saddle-bags, took out a handful of the money and showed it to the two men. He pointed at the spare horse, also equipped with saddle-bags.

"There's more there. You want to count it?"

Roper gave a lopsided grin. "Naw. If it ain't all okay when we take it to Red he'll know what to do with you." He drew a finger across his throat to signify graphically what Coogan might expect from The Butcher.

Coogan said nothing, but the warning sent a chill along his spine. He remembered what Sheene had done to the passengers on the stagecoach.

"So," Roper said, "let's go, huh?"

Coogan mounted up and they set off in the direction of the mountains. When they had travelled some distance Roper called a halt.

"What now?" Coogan asked.

"From here on in you gotta be blindfolded."

"Hell, no. That's not on the programme."

"Sure is. You don't think we're gonna show you the way in, do you?"

Coogan had thought it unlikely, but there had always been the chance. Now he saw that it was not to be. There was one grain of encouragement though: if they were being so careful not to let him see the way to their hideout it would seem to indicate that they intended he should come out again.

The Mexican had produced a gunny sack. Roper took the reins of his horse from Coogan's hands and Mex slipped the gunny sack over his head and pulled it down past his shoulders. It was a complete blindfold; he could now see nothing and was half stifled by the coarse sack which had a musty odour, as though whatever it had previously contained had gone mouldy before being emptied out.

They went on then, but at a somewhat slower pace, Roper leading Coogan's horse and Mex bringing up the rear with the spare mount in tow. Later Coogan could tell when they had left the grassland and were on less even ground. Here there seemed to be loose shale under the horses' hoofs and it was evident that they were going uphill, the slope becoming steeper as they progressed.

It was quite a while later when Roper gave the order to dismount. Coogan could still see nothing but he could hear Roper's voice.

"We gotta walk now. Mind your step."

"How can I mind my step when I can't see a thing?"

"You'll jest have to feel your way."

He heard the Mexican laugh.

The slope had become even steeper and Coogan had a feeling that they were on a narrow path. He kept one hand on the saddle of his horse and hoped the animal would not tread on his foot. Then he felt something flexible brushing against him like twigs or small branches, and after that the path levelled out and the air was noticeably cooler. Until then some light had been penetrating the coarse fabric of the sack, but now there appeared to be darkness all round and occasionally his left shoulder brushed against what

117

seemed to be a solid wall. He came to the conclusion that they had entered a tunnel and were perhaps moving into the heart of the mountain.

When light again became visible through the interstices of the sacking hood the path started on a downward slope which gradually flattened out. Soon after this Roper again called a halt and Coogan felt the gunny sack being lifted off. He blinked in the sudden daylight and saw the Mexican grinning at him, brown-stained teeth bared under the black moustache.

"Nearly home now," he growled.

Well, Coogan thought, it may be home for him but it certainly is not for me. But he took a look around to see what sort of a place they had come to anyway.

What he saw amazed him.

"My, oh, my!"

"Didn't expect this, huh?" Roper said.

"Sure didn't."

"You're privileged." Roper spoke

with a kind of mocking sneer. "Not many get the honour of being brung in here. And those as do often don't ever leave the place. Guess they just get kinda attached to it."

"I can imagine."

It was a valley apparently enclosed on all sides by walls of rock. In the centre was a lake shaped rather like a fat cigar, widest at the middle and tapering towards each end. The shores of the lake were for the most part wooded and much of the valley floor had a carpet of herbage, lush and green, with rocky outcrops here and there in various shapes and sizes. Horses were grazing on the pasture and the whole scene had an idyllic look about it.

Coogan's immediate thought was that it was far too good for a bunch of murderous villains like Butcher Sheene and his followers. They were like a blot on the fair face of nature and he wondered how they had stumbled on such a perfect retreat.

"That's where we live when we're at

home," Roper said.

Coogan saw that he was pointing towards one end of the valley where there was a huddle of buildings. At that distance it was difficult to tell for certain, but it looked as though they were made of stone, and again he was amazed. He could not believe that the Sheene gang had constructed such solid accommodation; a rough timber cabin or shack would have been the extent of their capabilities.

So who had done the building? Perhaps the same people who had fashioned the tunnel that gave access to the valley, or more likely had adapted a natural feature penetrating the narrow razor-backed ridge. But what had happened to those people? Had they died out years or even centuries ago? And had the valley remained undiscovered since then until Sheene and his desperadoes had lighted on it by chance and had realised its potential as a secret hideaway? Perhaps.

Roper had been watching him closely.

"Guess you're wondering what sort of place this is?"

"The thought did cross my mind."

"Come and see."

They were already almost halfway down the path which slanted down from the tunnel exit to the valley floor, and glancing back Coogan caught a glimpse of two men who were apparently keeping guard up there. Now with Roper going on ahead and Mex following behind he made his way down the path, the led horses going with them.

At the foot of the path they mounted up and rode towards the cluster of buildings half a mile or so away. As they drew nearer Coogan could see that these were largely in ruins, a fact which had not been apparent from a distance. But they had been solidly built and it was the roofing that had suffered most from the ravages of time and weather. They extended over a fairly wide area and in the distant past had no doubt constituted quite a large settlement.

"I reckon," Coogan said, "you lot must have taken over what somebody else built. Am I right?"

Roper gave a smirk. "You think we couldn't build a place like this?"

"Damn right, I do. You couldn't build a doll's house. You're destroyers, not constructors."

Roper's smirk faded. "Oh, sure, sure. But take my advice, pal. Don't go shootin off your mouth that way in front of Red."

"Why? Isn't it the truth?"

"Maybe it is at that. But maybe he don't like people to go around sounding off about the things he does. Maybe he'd think you was being kinda critical. And if there's one thing Red don't take to at all kindly it's criticism. Ain't that so, Mex?"

"You betcha," the Mexican said. He gave an evil grin. "Start anything like that with Red and hombre, you're in real trouble." He repeated the throat-slitting gesture with his dirty forefinger that Roper had made earlier. "One big knife, one big slice. Finish."

"Get the message, Brad?" Roger inquired.

"I get it," Coogan said.

Red Sheene was no glutton for criticism.

There were some men lounging around when the three horsemen rode in. Coogan could see more evidence now of how long the houses had been abandoned before Sheene's lot had taken them over. Grass and weeds had invaded the doorways, and in some of the buildings trees had taken root and were growing through the derelict roofs. The men hanging around cast curious glances at the new arrivals; it was evident that they knew why Coogan was there and they glanced greedily at the saddle-bags, maybe figuring in their heads what their share of the loot would be.

Roper led the way to a kind of village square with buildings on all sides and what looked like a well in the centre. Here he dismounted, Coogan and the

Mexican following suit. Roper called to a man who was sitting on the upper part of the well and whittling a stick with a clasp-knife.

"Seen Red around?"

"He was here a while back," the man said. "You got something for him?"

"Sure have."

"He'll be pleased," the whittler said.

At that moment a man stepped out from one of the houses which had had some crude repairs carried out on its roof. He stood in the doorway, hands on hips, gazing towards the little group in the square.

"Looking for me?" he shouted.

His voice was harsh, and Coogan needed no telling that here was the man he had been following all the way down from that home in Wyoming where the atrocities had taken place.

He looked at the man in the doorway and knew that this was Red Sheene, The Butcher.

He looked at Sheene and did not like what he saw.

7

SHEENE was really big; a monster in more senses than one. He must have been at least six and a half feet tall and close to three hundred pounds in weight. He had red hair and an unkempt beard, a nose that looked as though it had been squashed back into his face and a wide cruel mouth. His teeth were like a row of white palings in need of a fresh coat of paint, and there were gaps in them here and there.

He was wearing a battered old derby hat and a seaman's blue knitted jersey, buttoned on the left shoulder. His pants were made of some coarse grey cloth that looked as tough as sail-cloth and on his feet were scuffed rawhide boots with high heels. Circling his bulging waist was a gun-belt with a holstered six-shooter on the right-hand side. There was also a sheathed hunting-knife ready for use.

When he got a closer look at it Coogan could see that there were traces of dried blood on the handle of the knife, and he remembered Henry Makins's account of the slaughter in the stagecoach. There were some stains on the blue jersey that might also have been made by splashes of human blood. It was apparent that they did not bother Sheene.

He did not come to them; they had to go to him. He just crooked a forefinger and beckoned.

"Come on," Roper said. "He wants us."

They walked over to where Sheene was waiting, leading the horses. Sheene stared at Coogan for a few seconds and then spat.

"You bring the money?"

"Yes," Coogan said.

"Do I know you?"

"No, you don't know me. We've never met until now."

126

But I know you, Coogan was thinking. I know you, you murdering swine. He had an impulse to haul his gun out of the holster and pump its full load of bullets into that massive chest under the blue jersey. But he knew that this would be madness, an indulgence he could not afford. He had to play it cool.

"What's your name?" Sheene demanded.

"Brad."

"Just Brad? Nothing else?"

"Brad will do."

"Okay, Brad. You one of De Quincey's men?"

"No. I just happened to be at the ranch when this business came up."

"How come he sent you with the cash?"

"I offered to bring it."

"Why?"

Coogan shrugged. "Can't rightly say. Just a whim, I guess."

He thought Sheene looked suspicious, perhaps not wholly accepting this explanation.

127

"You get many whims like that?"

"No, not many."

"Maybe it's best for you if you don't. Could be bad for the health." He exploded suddenly in an immense guffaw that seemed to shake his whole body, vast chest heaving, belly quivering.

Roper and the Mexican joined in the laughter, like a pair of sycophants flattering their master. The amount of mirth generated seemed to be out of all proportion to the quality of the joke — if it was a joke; and from Coogan it failed to raise even the ghost of a smile.

Sheene's own laughter ceased abruptly, as though he had turned off a tap.

"So where is it?"

"The money, you mean?"

"Sure, the money. What else?"

"In the saddle-bags."

Sheene looked at Roper and the Mexican, who had stopped laughing immediately he had. "You counted it?"

"Naw," Roper said. "What the hell! We figured it'd all be there."

"You figured, did you? Okay, so now I figure you better take the damn bags and go count it. If you can count."

Roper looked sullen but made no retort. He removed the saddle-bags from Coogan's horse while the Mexican took those from the led animal. They walked away and entered one of the nearby houses.

"Scum!" Sheene said. He spat again.

Coogan gathered that he had a pretty low opinion of the two men. Perhaps they had a low opinion of him, too, but one thing he would have made a bet on was that they were scared of their leader. Even Mex, who looked as if he would not have feared anyone, man or devil, was cowed by Sheene. But maybe Sheene was both in one, and that was really something special.

"I think I'd better see the girl now," Coogan said.

Sheene gave an evil grin. "You wanna make sure she's all in one piece?"

"Something like that."

"Okay, Brad. You wanna see her, we'll go see her." He led the way to another of the houses that had had some work done on it in the way of repairs. It was quite a small building and there was a doorway at one end, but no door. One of the outlaws was lounging by the doorway, a limp cigarette in one corner of his mouth. He raised one hand in a kind of half-salute, which Sheene ignored. The big man had to stoop to get in through the opening and Coogan followed him inside.

There was only one room, light coming in through two small windows set high in the walls. The floor was pounded earth and there was little in the way of furniture. A rough wooden bunk with a kind of palliasse for a mattress and a couple of coarse grey blankets served for a bed.

On the bed was Miss Marian de Quincey.

She had been lying down, but she

sat up when Sheene and Coogan came in.

"You got a visitor," Sheene said. "Name's Brad. Know him?"

She glanced quickly at Coogan. She had perhaps been hoping to see a familiar face but was disappointed. She shook her head.

"No."

"He's from your paw. Says he's not one of the regular cowhands, just a volunteer for this job. He brung the ransom money."

"Ah!"

Coogan saw hope kindle in her eyes. And they were real nice eyes, he thought. De Quincey had said she was twenty-one but she looked younger; she could easily have passed for seventeen. And she was lovely, no doubt about that; with the fresh dewy beauty of the young that has no need of cosmetic aids. She looked vulnerable too.

"I've come to take you home, Miss De Quincey."

She stood up eagerly. "Now?"

131

Coogan glanced at Sheene. "That okay?"

"Now hold it," Sheene said. "The boys ain't finished counting the money yet. And where's the hurry? Shucks, it'll be dark soon. You'd lose your way. Better wait till morning."

The girl seemed to droop; the disappointment was apparent in her expression. She had obviously been thinking in terms of an immediate departure from her prison and that dream had been shattered by Sheene's words.

Coogan was disappointed too; and he detected a more sinister implication in the big man's suggestion. It might well be that he intended more than a mere postponement of the release of his hostage until morning; and now that he had the ransom money there was no way of forcing him to keep his side of the bargain. This was what Coogan had feared all along, but he had decided to take the risk. Now it began to look as if he had made a mistake in doing so.

Nevertheless, he did his best to persuade Sheene to change his mind. "Oh, we can find the way all right if we leave now. Plenty of daylight left for the start, and later there'll be a moon. You don't need to worry about us."

The words seemed to amuse Sheene and he gave a laugh. "Worry about you! Hell, no. You must be crazy if you think I got the time to do that."

"So we can go straightaway?"

"No. Fact is I've taken a liking to you, Brad. Don't get many visitors here and I'd like to show you my kingdom."

"Your kingdom?"

"That's what I call this valley."

"You own it?"

"Well, it's a cinch nobody else does. Me and the boys took it over; we occupy it and I guess that gives us the right to it. And me, I'm the bossman around here, as you may have noticed."

"Yes, I had noticed," Coogan answered drily.

"So I reckon as how that makes me king."

Coogan looked into Sheene's eyes and read a hint of something there which chilled his blood. It was madness. He had no doubt about it in his own mind. And if Sheene were mad that made him completely unpredictable and utterly without conscience. Perhaps he really did believe he was a king, with the divine right that kingship bestowed.

"How did you find the way in here in the first place?" he asked. "Other people have looked, but without success."

"Luck," Sheene said. "Sheer luck. There was this mountain goat we was tryin' to get a shot at. It went up the side of the mountain and suddenly disappeared. We followed it and found the tunnel it had gone inside."

"So a goat showed you the way?"

"That's about the size of it. Reckon somebody up there's looking after us." Sheene pointed a finger upward, leering.

Coogan pointed at the floor. "Or

down there. They say the Devil looks after his own."

Sheene was not in the least put out by this suggestion. He still grinned. "One or the other. Makes no difference which."

At that moment Roper appeared in the doorway.

"You finished counting the money?" Sheene asked.

"Yeah. All correct. Twenty thousand."

"Good." Sheene turned to the girl. "That daddy of yours must think the world of you, honey. Coughed up the dollars real pronto. Must be a mighty rich man, too. Plenty more where that lot come from. I guess?"

The girl said nothing.

Again Coogan had the feeling that he could read what was passing in Sheene's mind. Mad or not, he was greedy for money, and the ease with which twenty thousand dollars had fallen into his hands might simply have persuaded him to go for more. And he still had the means to extract it. He still held Miss Marian De Quincey.

He dismissed Roper with a wave of the hand. Then he spoke to Coogan. "Let's you and me go take a ride."

Coogan saw that argument was useless; it might only serve to anger the man. But before leaving he had a word with the girl.

"Are you all right?"

She gave a little nod.

"They haven't mistreated you?"

"No."

Sheene gave a laugh. "It's okay, Brad. We bin looking after her real dandy. The goods ain't damaged at all. So far."

Coogan did not care for those last two words. They contained a threat, only thinly veiled. There could be no doubt that as long as she was held in captivity Miss De Quincey presented a powerful temptation not only to Sheene but to every man in his gang of desperadoes. He wondered whether she realised it; and he had little doubt that she did.

But for the present there was nothing he could do about it.

★ ★ ★

The settlement was at the upper end of the valley, which at its widest was some three-quarters of a mile across and was perhaps a couple of miles in length. As they rode Sheene and Coogan had the lake on their right, and in places they threaded their way through the trees which grew along its shores.

Sheene was mounted on a big grey horse which reminded Coogan of the sight he had had of a band of riders in the moonlight led by a huge man on just such a steed. He had no doubt whatever now that that man had been Sheene.

And now this same Red Sheene was taking him on a conducted tour of what he chose to call his kingdom. It was strange the way things had worked out, and he was puzzled as to why the man should be doing this. Could it be that he took a warped kind of pride in this piece of land that he had grabbed and made his own? Was he delighted to take his chance of showing it off to someone from the outside? He had said he did not have many visitors.

"Nice place, ain't it?" Sheene remarked. He had come to a halt at a spot where the lake was bordered by a shingly beach, and Coogan had drawn his horse up beside him. "Real nice, I'd say."

Coogan was amazed that a man like Sheene should have been moved to express so much appreciation of the scene. There could be no doubt about the beauty of that shimmering stretch of water with the background of woods and mountains reflected in its limpid mirror, but that this murderous villain could be impressed by it came as a surprise; it revealed another wildly contrasting side of his character; for it was obvious that he did genuinely admire the natural splendour of the view.

And yet the man was a monster.

"Yes," Coogan agreed. "Very nice."

And it occurred to him that he might kill the monster then and there. It was a measure of Sheene's overweening self-assurance that he had not bothered to disarm Coogan; that he had ridden alone in his company with all the confidence in the world. And now he, Coogan had only to draw his revolver and shoot, and that would be the end of Sheene for good and all. It would not be murder; it would be an execution.

He thought about it, and his hand itched to grasp the butt of the gun; but if he had been going to do it he should have done so without thinking; because while he hesitated the arguments against such a course of action came flooding into his mind. Killing Sheene would not solve every problem. True, he would be dead, but his gang of villains would still be very much alive, and they had Miss De Quincey in their hands. Even if he could have escaped with his own life, which was doubtful, he could have done so only by abandoning the girl and proving himself unworthy of the trust placed in him by her father. It just could not be done.

He heard Sheene give a chuckle. "You won't do it, you know."

Coogan glanced at him, startled. The man must have been reading his mind. And once again Sheene had demonstrated the ability to surprise him; this time by the acuteness of his intuition.

"You thought maybe you'd kill me, didn't you? And then you thought some more and it didn't seem such a hot idea after all. Wouldn't have done you no good, would it?"

"At least you'd have been dead."

"Maybe. If I hadn't been quicker on the draw than you. Look."

Sheene gave a demonstration. The gun seemed to leap from its holster into his hand. It was like a conjuring trick. Coogan knew that he could not have matched it.

Sheene chuckled again and put the gun back in the leather. "Let's go."

Coogan went with him, chastened.

Near the end of the valley the lake narrowed to a stream, and fifty yards farther on the stream plunged into a hole in the wall of rock that now confronted the riders, splashing and gurgling as it went. Coogan dismounted, stepped on to a flattened boulder in the bed of the stream and peered into the opening. He could see only a few yards; beyond that all was dark.

Sheene watched him with obvious amusement. "Wouldn't be thinking that was another way out of the valley, would you, Brad?"

"If it is," Coogan said, "I still think I'd prefer the way I came in."

On the ride back he brought up the subject of who had constructed the buildings at the upper end of the valley.

"Got any thoughts on that?"

"Sure, I have," Sheene replied. "My guess is they was Indians."

"I thought Indians lived in wigwams."

"Common idea," Sheene said, "but not entirely correct. I was talking to a man once that had studied the subject. He said the Indians was all descended from Asiatics who crossed over into America centuries ago up north. Then they filtered south, splitting up into various tribes with different cultures. Some of 'em built wooden houses and the like, and those as got right down into Mexico built pyramids and stone houses and all that. So my guess is the ones that came into this valley knew how to build in stone or learnt to while they was here. I think maybe they was just a small tribe and this was their stronghold."

"So what happened to them? You think they were finally defeated and killed?"

"More likely they just died from some plague. We found a lot of skeletons."

It sounded unlikely to Coogan. Maybe some European settlers pushing west had used the place as a stronghold against the Indians. But who could tell? One thing was certain: Sheene knew a lot more about Indians than he himself did. He had never known that they came originally from Asia; had thought of them simply as a bunch of bloodthirsty savages. Well, you lived and learned, even from a monster like Sheene. He felt somewhat humbled to realise that Sheene knew a deal more on some subjects than he did.

But he still intended to kill the man. It was what he had come all this way to do and he had no intention of abandoning his purpose.

It was growing dusk when they arrived back at the settlement and the air was cool. A fire had been lighted in the square not far from the well and a side of beef was being barbecued over it. Coogan suspected that the beef had originally been one of De Quincey's steers grazing on the Circle Q pasture.

He had seen no cattle in the valley.

He and Sheene dismounted and the gang boss ordered one of his men to lead the horses away and attend to their needs. The man went off with the mounts and at that moment another man stepped out from one of the nearby houses and walked towards the fire. Sheene glanced at him as he came into the flickering light of the flames.

"I thought you was sick," he said. "Why ain't you lyin' down?"

The man looked sick. There was a dirty bandage on his right forearm and it could have been the wound that was making him ill. Possibly it was festering, and Coogan would not have been surprised if this had been so, because Doc Lawson had seemed to him to be half drunk when he had dressed the wound in the Pikeville cell, and not much concerned with the matter of medical hygiene.

Not that it was the man's health that was giving Coogan any cause for alarm; he would have shed no tears if the invalid had died on the spot, indeed, it would have given him great pleasure to see this happen. For the fact was that it was the mere presence of this particular person in this particular place at this particular time that really bothered him.

He could have wished Ben Krane to be anywhere else in the whole wide world at that moment than the place where he did indeed happen to be. Because if there was one thing Krane could be trusted to bring with him it was trouble for one, Brad Coogan; trouble of the worst possible kind.

8

"OH, I'm sick all right," Krane said, "but not half as sick as this bastard is gonna be. Do you know who he is?"

"Sure, I know," Sheene said. "Name's Brad."

"Yes, but do you know who Brad is? That's the question."

"What in hell are you talkin' about?" Sheene sounded impatient. "What're you drivin' at? He's the one what brung the ransom money from De Quincey."

"Ah, that's what they told me. They said his name was Brad and I got to thinking. I didn't believe it could be the same Brad, but it is. This here is Brad Coogan, the swine that shot Art and Joe and put a slug in my arm."

"You're crazy. You're light-headed. You're just imaginin' things."

"No, I'm not. I'd know that face in a million. That's him."

Krane was stabbing his finger at Coogan, and Coogan could see all too clearly now the way it had been. Those riders he and Lois had seen in the moonlight with the big man leading had indeed been Sheene and his gang. And of course they had been on their way to Pikeville to spring Krane from his cell. In fact the thought had crossed his mind at the time, but he had dismissed it because he could think of no way Sheene could have known that Krane was under arrest.

Thinking about it now, however, the answer suddenly came to him with blinding clarity: Loder. He remembered the horseman galloping off into the night and Deputy Luke Mackley telling him that the sheriff had been called away on urgent business. Well, it was plain enough now what that business had been. Loder was in cahoots with the Sheene gang; he knew where they hung out and he had made haste to tell them that their man Krane was under lock and key in Pikeville. So then they had come to break him out. There was no doubt in Coogan's mind now that that was the way it had happened.

And now he really was in trouble, because he could see that Sheene was beginning to believe Krane was telling the truth.

"So," Sheene said in a musing kind of way, stroking his beard and gazing at Coogan, "you're Brad Coogan."

Coogan thought of denying it, thought of protesting that Krane had got it all wrong and that his name was Smith or Brown or something. But he knew it would be useless; he would not be believed. So he said nothing.

"And it was you killed two of my boys. That was bad, real bad."

"They got what was coming to them," Coogan said.

"You had something against them?"

"You bet I had. Like I've got something against you, Sheene, and against the whole stinking tribe of you."

"Ah!" Sheene said; speaking softly, staring at Coogan, not moving. "And what would that something be?"

"The death of my wife and daughter. The wrecking of my home."

"Where's your home, Coogan?"

"You should say where was it? Up in Wyoming. But no more; never again. That's all gone because of you."

"Yes," Sheene said, still in that musing way, not raising his voice, "we was up in them parts a while back. Having us a whale of a time. So you bin trailing us, have you? Figurin' as how you'd take revenge maybe?"

"Right in one, Butcher."

The name appeared to sting Sheene. Perhaps no one had dared to use it to his face before. His eyes glittered in the firelight.

"And you finally caught up with us. Good for you, Coogan. Only not so good for you. Better for you if you'd never come within a hundred miles of us. 'Cos you're a dead man, Coogan; do you know that? A dead man."

Coogan's hand dropped to the butt of his revolver. Maybe it was true that he was a dead man, but he would make sure he was not the only one; he would kill Sheene now and his quest would be completed. That was how it would be; the two of them would go together.

His fingers tightened on the butt and he had already lifted the gun half out of the holster when he was seized from behind by two men, each grabbing an arm. He tried to break free but it was no use; they were both strong and they had the advantage. A third man took the revolver from him, and now there was no way he could harm Sheene, no way he could take the bandit leader with him when he made that last long journey into darkness.

Sheene drew the hunting-knife from its sheath and showed it to Coogan, gloatingly. "Reckon you made one big mistake when you volunteered for that there courier job. You should've let some other stupid bastard bring the money. But no; you had to push yourself forward, and now look where it's got you. See this knife?"

"I see it," Coogan said. He could not help seeing it, or the dried blood which he knew had come from human throats. Soon no doubt there would be fresh stains on the blade, because it was a dead cert that Sheene intended using it again. Soon.

"Butcher, you called me. Well, we know what butchers do, don't we? They cut pigs' throats. And if I'm the butcher, Mister Coogan, it's a cinch you're the pig."

He gave a nod to the man who had taken Coogan's gun, and the man swept Coogan's hat from his head, grabbed a handful of hair and jerked the head back so that the throat was exposed, skin stretched tight over the Adam's apple.

Krane was loving it; he could not keep still. Coogan guessed that he would have liked to do the killing himself; but that was Sheene's prerogative and Krane would not have dared to take it from him. He had to be content with urging his leader on.

"That's the way, Red. Give it to him. Slice his gullet. Make him bleed."

Sheene glanced at him. "You reckon I should?"

Krane seemed taken aback by the question. "What else, boss?"

Sheene tested the sharpness of the blade with the ball of his left thumb, as if to make sure it was up to the job. "Well now, it's like this; I have to look at all the angles. That's because I am the boss, see? You don't even have to use your brains, because all you have to do is what I tell you. Am I right?"

Krane looked at him uncertainly, not getting the drift. "Well, sure, Red, sure."

"And by your reckoning I should slit this here throat? Right?"

"Right," Krane said; but again he seemed uncertain, unable to see what Sheene was getting at.

"Ah well, maybe you're on the mark at that. Maybe I oughter do it. He killed two of my boys, didn't he?"

"That's so, Red. Shot 'em dead. And he did this to me an' all." Krane showed his bandaged arm, his voice shrill with indignation.

"So he did, so he did. But you musta bin slow on the uptake to let him do that. I mean to say there was three of you and only one of him. So how come?"

"Aw, he had the drop on us." Krane spoke sulkily. "Didn't give us a chance."

"Now that really was bad of him. Didn't give you a chance, huh?" There was mockery in Sheene's voice, and Krane shifted from one foot to the other, not liking it. "Man should always give another man a chance. You would, wouldn't you, Ben?"

Krane said nothing. Coogan wondered what Sheene's object was in spinning things out. Maybe it was just a bit of mental torture; playing with his victim as a cat would play with a mouse; keeping him on tenterhooks waiting for the knife. He was baiting Krane, but it was Coogan he was really putting on the rack.

But he seemed to tire of it. "Well," he said, "this won't get the cows to market. And that beef sure smells good."

Coogan could also smell the odour of roasting meat, and it made him aware of his own hunger. But there was little point in thinking about that in his present situation, because there was no record of a man ever enjoying a hearty meal with his throat cut. Not that he had heard of.

And then the cold steel blade touched his neck, and it sent a shiver through his whole body. He felt it slide across the stretched skin and he knew that this was where for him the curtain fell.

But it was not. The blade went just deep enough to draw a thread of blood like a ruby necklace below his chin and was then withdrawn.

"No," Sheene said. "Why be hasty?"

Krane stared at him. "You mean you

ain't going to do it?"

"No. At least not for the present. The time will come but it ain't now."

"For God's sake, why not? Gimme the knife; I'll do it. I got one good hand; that'll be enough."

"Shut your mouth." Sheene made a kind of flick with his left hand and struck Krane on the side of the jaw. For him it probably rated as the lightest of blows, no more than a tap, but it staggered Krane and he almost fell. "You talk too much. All talk and no think, that's you. Me, I use my nut and work things out in here." He touched the side of his forehead with a thick finger. "And I say to myself, where's the sense in cutting our Mr Coogan's throat when I still got a job for him to do? It's pretty damn sure he won't be doing a thing bar pushing up daisies if he's got a gap in his throttle. Savvy?"

Krane mumbled something and massaged his jaw, which was probably still sore from the knock Coogan had given him with the rifle butt. For a moment there had been a glitter in his eyes, and he might have killed Sheene then if he had had a gun. But he was unarmed and the glitter died out as quickly as it had come and he became subservient again.

Hope was reborn in Coogan as he heard Sheene's words. What job it was that the man had in mind he could not guess, but if it would save his life he did not care what it was. He had as much desire to live as the next man, and the fact that he had been so close to death made life seem all the sweeter. He waited for Sheene to explain what it was he had to do, but the gang leader was not yet ready to divulge the information.

Sheene slipped the hunting-knife back in its sheath and spoke to the two men still holding Coogan.

"Take him to the ladder."

Coogan wondered what was meant by 'the ladder', but he was not left long in ignorance. The two men, each still holding one of his arms, marched him away to a place where a couple of stout posts about eight feet tall were embedded in the ground. The posts were some six feet apart and were connected to each other by half a dozen cross-pieces nailed to the uprights. This was the ladder.

The men stripped him to the waist and pushed him up against the ladder facing the steps, to which they tied his wrists and ankles so that he was spreadeagled on the framework as though crucified. It began to dawn on him now what was going to happen next, and when Sheene ordered Roper to fetch the whip he could no longer have any doubt.

He was to be scourged.

Roper hurried away to do his master's bidding and was back within the minute, bringing a heavy stock-whip with him. This he handed to Sheene.

Sheene made the whip crack in the

air like a pistol shot. He spoke to Coogan.

"You know what happens now, don't you?"

"I can guess. But why?"

"Punishment. You killed my boys. For that you gotta die, but not yet. This is just to be going on with. A taster, as you might say. After this you won't need no reminding you're living on a short lease. You'll feel it in the back and it'll tell you the real sentence has just been postponed. It'll tell you that some day, before long, the knife will be at your throat again, and next time it'll dig deep, real deep. You're still a dead man, Coogan."

As he spoke the last word the lash snaked out. Coogan's body quivered as he felt the bite of it on his back and it was all he could do to choke back a cry of pain. It was like the sting of a hornet, but very much worse. He waited for the next stroke and heard Sheene give a grunt as he sent the leather hissing through the air a second time.

It was worse than the first. Perhaps initially Sheene had just been getting the range and now had it accurately to the fraction of an inch. Coogan clenched his teeth and again held back any cry. Though he could have screamed with the agony of the lash, which he guessed must be cutting through the skin, he refused to give Sheene that satisfaction.

By turning his head he could see out of the corner of his eye the men gathered in a bunch to watch the whipping and no doubt enjoy this torture of a fellow human being. He cursed them in his heart and wished them all consigned to hell-fire; but most of all he cursed that villainous giant with the whip.

Again the leather hissed and cracked. Again he shuddered under the impact, writhing in a useless effort to break free; the cords simply cut more deeply into his wrists and he was powerless to avoid the lash which came again and again. He could hear the outlaws jeering and laughing, urging Sheene on. It was a show to them, something to whet the appetite before they sank their teeth into the roasted beef.

It seemed to go on for an age. Coogan was drowning in a sea of pain and it appeared to him that Sheene would never tire. But tired or not, he called a halt to the torture at last. If, as he had said, he had a job for Coogan there would have been no sense in crippling or even killing his man. Not that he had desisted by any means too soon from the victim's point of view. Coogan could not see his back, but he knew that it must be in a mess; he could feel blood from the weals left by the whip trickling down to his waist and the entire area of misused skin felt as though it were on fire.

Sheene was breathing hard as he coiled the whip, and he spoke jeeringly. "How're you feelin' now, Coogan? Has that warmed you up some?"

160

Coogan said nothing.

"What's wrong with you? Lost your tongue?"

Still Coogan made no reply.

"Well," Sheene said, "if you don't wanna talk, don't. I ain't wasting any more time on you. Got some eatin' to do."

He came back later and stood on the other side of the frame where Coogan could see him through the bars. He had a great hunk of roast beef in one hand a bottle of whisky in the other, and he stood there alternately chewing the meat with the juices dribbling down his beard and taking swigs of whisky from the bottle.

"You hungry, Coogan?" he asked.

"Go to hell," Coogan said.

Sheene laughed. "So you found your tongue again. And there was me thinking you'd bin struck dumb. Like some meat? Ask me nice and I might give you some."

Coogan relapsed into silence.

"No?" Sheene said. "Well, I'm a

161

generous man, so maybe I'll give you some anyway."

He came up close to the frame and pushed the remains of the beef he had been chewing into Coogan's face. Coogan felt nauseated and kept his mouth shut.

"Go on," Sheene urged. "Take a bite."

Still Coogan refused to open his mouth.

"Aw," Sheene said, "I see what it is. You don't like eatin' after me. You got fancy tastes, I guess. Maybe I disgust you with my table manners."

Coogan broke his silence. "You can say that again. You make me sick. I'd rather share a trough with a herd of hogs."

He had the limited satisfaction of seeing that his words had goaded Sheene, though he was to pay for this small triumph. Sheene smeared his face with the juicy meat, spat at him and slouched away.

★ ★ ★

162

It was a cool night and Coogan was left to endure the cold still tied to the so-called ladder. He felt the pain in his back and the chill in his whole body. He shivered uncontrollably and was hungry and thirsty. Yet he had to endure it, for he had no choice; all he could do was wait for the dawn of another day and any good that it might bring.

He had no idea what time it was when he heard the woman's voice. The fire had died down and the men had all gone long since, no doubt to sleep soundly after the heavy meal which they had not shared with him.

The woman said: "Are you asleep?"

His eyes had been closed but he had not been sleeping; the pain and the cold made sleep an impossibility. Now he turned his head and saw the woman standing beside him, shadowy in the moonlight. For a moment he thought perhaps he was asleep and this was a dream.

"Who are you?" he asked.

163

"My name is Rachel."

He was bewildered, still only half-believing that she was flesh and blood and not a phantom of his own imagining. "I don't understand. How do you come to be here?"

She answered simply: "This is where I live."

In that light it was difficult to judge her age, but he felt sure she was not young. Though not old, either.

"You live here? With these — "

"With these men? Yes; I am their woman."

He detected the bitterness in her voice and guessed that she had not willingly given herself to them. Her next words told him that he was right.

"They took me," she said. "Five years ago. They killed my husband but spared my life and took me with them. Perhaps it would have been better if they had killed me as well. Sometimes I have thought of killing myself, but I lack the courage. And there is another thing; I want to live to see these wretches pay for their crimes. I wait for that day; I pray for it; but it has been a long time in coming."

"Perhaps," Coogan said, "it will not be so long now." And even as he said it he thought what empty words they must seem to her, coming as they did from a man in his perilous situation. For what could he do to speed the day?

"I have brought you some food," she said. "I had to wait until they were all asleep."

"Did you bring a knife to cut me free?" he asked.

She shook her head. "I didn't dare. They would know I did it. And what use would it be? There are guards at the tunnel. and there is no other way out of the valley."

"But if I have to stay tied like this how can I feed myself?"

"You won't need to. I will feed you."

She had brought a kind of stew which she fed to him with a spoon, and a pot of coffee and a tin mug from which he drank. When his hunger and thirst had been satisfied she examined his back as closely as she could in the moonlight.

"It is bad," she said, "but I have seen worse. He treated you lightly."

"Lightly! It didn't feel like it."

"By his standards it was. He has flogged men to death. He must want to keep you alive."

"He does. He has a job for me."

"What kind of job?"

"I don't know. I can only guess that it has to do with Miss De Quincey."

"Ah, that poor girl," Rachel said. "I wonder what will happen to her."

"I was supposed to take her home."

"But you think it will not happen like that now?"

"I doubt whether Sheene intends to let her go. For the present at least."

She noticed that he was shivering. "You are cold. I would fetch a blanket to cover you, but again they would know who had taken pity on you. I am sorry."

"It doesn't matter. What time is it?"

"Long past midnight."

"Then I haven't many more hours to endure. And I thank you for your kindness."

She went away soon after that, and he thought how wretched for her life must have been in those five long years in which she had been a slave to these men. She had not said whether she had had any children and if the outlaws had killed them too. Perhaps she had suffered more than he had; perhaps she had even more to avenge.

9

HE was thankful to see the first grey light of dawn; it told him that his present ordeal might soon be coming to an end. Yet it was still some time before he could detect any signs of life around the place. He was chilled to the bone and his back was giving him considerable pain.

It was the Mexican who eventually came to him. The Mexican stood with his legs apart and hands on hips regarding him with a mocking grin.

"You sleep well, gringo?"

"What do you think?"

"Me, I think you look like a man got himself a rough time. You don't look so good."

"I don't feel so good."

"No? You be better if you don't come looking for trouble. You look for trouble, you get trouble. Better to keep your head down."

"Thanks for the advice," Coogan said. "A bit late, but better late than never, so they say. Are you going to cut me free or do I have to stay here for ever?"

"No. There's job for you."

"So I heard. What job would that be?"

"Red tell you."

The Mexican took a knife from its sheath and severed the bonds that were holding Coogan's ankles and wrists. He could scarcely move; his entire body seemed to be frozen stiff. Gradually, however, he coaxed some life back into his limbs and the joints became workable again. The Mexican handed him his shirt and when he put it on it chafed the weals on his back as though it had been made of sandpaper. The pain ran through him like a prairie fire and he winced.

The Mexican grinned again. He seemed to spend half his time grinning. He was lucky to find so much fun in life.

"Bad back?"

"Damned bad."

"Will heal. You come now, get some grub."

He led the way to one of the houses where most of the men were seated at a long table of rough boards eating their breakfast. Coogan and the Mexican joined them. There was a wood fire. burning on a hearth and Coogan saw that the woman who had come to him in the night was cooking on it and serving the men. He could see her more plainly now, and she seemed more careworn than had been apparent in the moonlight. She might have been a good-looker once, but she had had a hard time and it showed.

She avoided looking at him, and it was evident that she did not wish to catch his eye or to give the slightest hint that she had had any contact with him. He could well understand this reluctance and played his own part by doing nothing which might indicate that he was acquainted with her in any way.

170

Sheene was not there; possibly he had already breakfasted or had other business to attend to. It was not until half an hour later that Roper came to tell Coogan that the boss wanted to see him.

"Where is he?" Coogan asked.

"Come with me. I'll take you to him."

Sheene was in the house where Miss De Quincey was being held captive. She was looking very depressed, and Coogan wondered what Sheene had been saying to her. She glanced quickly at him when he came in with Roper and a flicker of hope came into her eyes, but he gave a shake of the head and her shoulders drooped.

"I been givin' the young lady here a report on the state of the game," Sheene said. "She don't seem too happy about it."

"What is the state of the game?" Coogan asked.

"Well, it's like this: missie's gotta stay here a bit longer. She don't like

171

it, but that's the way it is." He looked at the girl and gave an evil grin. "Don't worry, sweetheart; we'll take care of you real good; never fear."

It was obvious that this assurance did nothing to allay her fears. She seemed to shrink away from him and her face was pallid.

"Why does she have to stay here?" Coogan demanded. "According to the bargain you should let her go now. You've got the ransom money."

Sheene stroked his beard. "I got some of it."

"What do you mean? It was all there. Twenty thousand dollars. That was the price."

"Oh, sure, it was the price," Sheene said. "But it ain't now. Not any more."

"Why not?"

"It ain't enough; that's why."

"It was what you asked for. You named the figure."

"True. But I see now I was robbing myself."

"So now what do you want?"

"Let's say another twenty thousand. I guess old man De Quincey can afford it."

It was what Coogan had suspected. Having found it so easy to get what he had demanded in the first place, Sheene had decided to raise the stakes. It was not honest, but when had honesty been any part of the make-up of such a man?

Sheene spoke to the girl. "What do you think, missie? Does your daddy love you enough to cough up the extra?"

She said nothing; she just looked beaten.

"Well," Sheene said, "never mind what you think. My guess is he will. And you, Coogan, are going to take the message to him. Another twenty thousand if he wants to see his darling daughter ever again."

"So that's the job you had for me?"

"That's it. And you're to bring the cash."

"Why me?"

"Because I say so."

Coogan could see how it was. Sheene wanted him back; maybe to give him another whipping; maybe to carry out the throat-slitting that had been postponed this time. And if he got the second twenty thousand what was to prevent him from still hanging on to the girl and demanding even more? The game could go on indefinitely and still end in Miss De Quincey remaining in the hands of her kidnappers to do with as they pleased.

It was one hell of a situation.

But for him there was no choice; for what would be gained by refusing to carry the message to De Quincey? Sheene would get it to the rancher by some other means and he, Coogan, would soon be out of the reckoning for good and all.

"Okay," he said. "When do I start?"

* * *

Roper and the Mexican accompanied him out of the valley. They put the gunny sack over his head before they entered the tunnel and they were halfway to Black Rock before they took it off. They kept him company as far as the rock and there had been no sign of anyone else around, just rolling grassland with the mountains looming in the distance behind them.

"Well," Roper said, "this is where we part company. Reckon we'll be seeing you again, Coogan."

"Reckon you will."

"But don't try anything smart. You might get hurt."

"I did get hurt. Perhaps you didn't notice."

"Next time it could be worse."

The Mexican grinned.

"So long," Roper said.

He and the Mexican turned their horses and started on the return journey. They did not look back.

Coogan had just his own horse; Sheene had kept the spare one. Perhaps he figured that it would be ready for Miss De Quincey to ride when she was eventually released; but more likely he guessed that her father would send another one when the second lot of money was delivered. He seemed confident that De Quincey would not refuse to pay up.

Coogan had been riding for another half-hour when he fell in with a handful of De Quincey's men under the leadership of Steve Devon, the foreman. They appeared surprised to see him.

"So it's you, Coogan," Devon said. "Damned if I ever expected to see you again."

"Why not?"

"When you didn't come back with Miss De Quincey the general opinion was that you'd hightailed it with the twenty thousand dollars."

"And you shared that opinion?"

"Guess so."

"How about Mr De Quincey? Did he think I'd done a bunk with the cash?"

"Don't know what he thought. But he had parties out looking for you. And he got in touch with Sheriff Van Doren and asked him to help. But nobody found hide nor hair of you."

"Been amazing if they had."

"So what happened to you?"

"A hell of a lot. But I think I'll keep it for Mr De Quincey's ears. He's the one most concerned."

Devon seemed none too pleased with this answer. He was naturally curious to hear Coogan's story. But all he said was: "You don't look none too chipper to me. Lost your guns too, I see."

"Yes, lost my guns too."

Devon asked no more questions and the journey back to the ranch-house was a silent one. Coogan sensed a feeling of hostility in the attitude of the foreman and the cowboys, and he guessed that they still had suspicions about him. At the very least it was likely that they held him to blame for the lack of success in getting Miss

De Quincey out of the clutches of the outlaws.

De Quincey was at the ranch-house and he looked grim when he saw Coogan. He took him straight into the room where he had received him and his two companions on the occasion of their first meeting, telling Devon to accompany them. There was no sign of Hanning or Lois Lloyd.

"Now," he said, "tell me all about it."

Coogan told him in as few words as possible; and as he recounted what had happened the rancher's frown steadily deepened. It was apparent to Coogan that he was both angry and worried; as was only to be expected.

"So," he said, when Coogan had come to the end of the story, "that villain intends to extort more money out of me?"

"I'm afraid so."

"And my daughter? How is she?"

"She seems well. Frightened, of course, and very unhappy, but reasonably well in the circumstances."

"They haven't — " De Quincey hesitated, as though unable to bring himself to formulate the question that was in his mind; perhaps fearful of what the answer might be. But he braced himself and went on. "They haven't maltreated her in any way?"

"So far, no."

"So far! Then you think they may do so?"

"I don't know what they may do. I just know they're a set of unscrupulous devils who'll stop at nothing. And Sheene is the worst of the bunch. He may even be mad."

"And you say he flogged you?"

"Yes."

"Why did he do that?"

"He called it punishment — for killing two of his men. I'm sure he would have killed me if he hadn't needed me as a go-between. He did this to show me what could happen to me another time." Coogan touched his throat where the cut was visible as a thin line, the blood dried on it.

"I owe you an apology," De Quincey said.

"For what?"

"When you did not return I suspected you had taken the money and ridden away. Instead you were risking your life, as you must have known when you went with those two men."

"Think no more about it. The question is what to do now. Will you pay the extra money?"

"I must. I have no alternative."

"It will be sending good money after bad."

"What do you mean?"

"I mean Sheene will simply demand more. He will go on doing that until you have nothing left to send him. And still you won't have your daughter back."

There was an anguished expression on De Quincey's face. "Do you really believe that?"

"I'm sure of it. I feel certain in my

own mind that he has no intention of letting her go."

"Oh, my God!" The man's distress was painful to observe. "What are we to do? What can we do?" He was appealing to Coogan, begging him to provide a solution to this insuperable problem.

Coogan said: "As I see it, there is only one course of action to take if we are to have any hope of success. We must storm the hideout and rescue your daughter by force."

De Quincey made a gesture of impatience and spoke petulantly. "Now you are talking nonsense. To storm the stronghold we have to get into it. And we don't know the way in. You have been in and out, but you say they blindfolded you. Isn't that so?"

"Certainly it is."

"Therefore you have no knowledge of where the entrance is and the plan is hopeless."

"It's true," Coogan admitted, "that I don't know the way in. But there is a man who does."

De Quincey glanced at him sharply. "What man is that?"

"Sheriff Loder of Pikeville."

"Loder! But how would he know?"

"It's my guess that he's in league with Sheene."

De Quincey showed his disbelief. "Have you any evidence to support that improbable idea?"

Coogan told him what had made him suspect Loder: the fact that Krane had been removed from custody, the riders in the night going in the direction of Pikeville and returning later.

De Quincey shook his head doubtfully, not fully convinced. "It doesn't prove Loder was implicated."

"But who else could have tipped Sheene off to the fact that Krane was behind bars in Pikeville? And I had it from Deputy Luke Mackley that Loder went off on some urgent business in the night. He didn't get back until late the next day."

De Quincey looked at Devon. "What

do you think, Steve?"

The foreman scratched his chin. "I reckon Mr Coogan could be right. I've had some dealings with Sheriff Loder and it's my opinion he's as crooked as a dog's hind leg."

De Quincey walked to the window and stared out. He came back and stood in front of the fireplace with the flint-lock muskets and the muzzle-loading pistols hanging on the wall behind him. He seemed a prey to uncertainty.

"Even if, as you suspect, Loder does know the way into the outlaws' den, how do we get the information from him? You may be sure he'll admit to nothing that would implicate himself."

"Leave that to me," Coogan said. "Just let me have some of your men and I'll guarantee to get the information."

"I suppose I'd better not ask how you intend doing that?"

"Do you really want to know?"

"No," De Quincey said, "I don't."

"If it's okay with you, sir," Devon

said, "I'd like to go with Mr Coogan."

De Quincey signified his agreement with a nod. "And you'd better pick the men you want. Take as many as you need." He turned to Coogan. "When will you go to Pikeville?"

"I think we should make a start this evening. Then we'll be there soon enough to make a start before dawn. There's going to be a lot of riding to do."

"You'd better warn the men, Steve," De Quincey said.

Devon said he would do that.

"And I'll need an hour or two of shuteye," Coogan said. "I didn't catch any sleep last night and I'm plumb tuckered out."

He had hardly got to the room allotted to him when the door opened again and Miss Lloyd walked in, not bothering to knock.

"Oh," she said, "they told me you were back." Then she noticed his neck and he could hear her sharp intake of breath. "That cut! Who did it?"

"Sheene. It was something on account of what he's promised to deliver later. If he hadn't had a use for me I'd have been dead meat by now."

"Oh God!" she said. "I had a feeling something bad had happened to you. They said you'd skipped with the money, but I told them you wouldn't do a thing like that; I just knew you wouldn't."

"Well, thanks, Lois. I'm glad somebody had faith in me. What did Matt think?"

"He said he didn't believe it either. He said you wanted to take revenge on Sheene too badly to be diverted by anything, including twenty thousand dollars."

"Matt's a pretty shrewd son-of-a-gun. I wonder what he would have done in my place."

"He wondered that himself. I don't think he could be sure of the answer."

When she saw Coogan's back she drew her breath in sharply again. "Oh, Brad! Oh, my dear!"

"It's not as bad as it looks," Coogan said. But he knew it was.

She fetched warm water and bathed the cuts and smeared on some kind of soothing ointment. Then she bandaged him with cloth torn from a sheet; and only when this was done did she allow him to lie face downward on the bed and catch up on some of that sleep he was so much in need of.

"I shall go to Pikeville with you, of course."

He did not attempt to argue with her. He knew it would have been useless and he was too damned tired anyway. Less than a minute after lying down he was asleep.

10

THEY travelled at an easy pace to save the horses. Pikeville was dark and silent when they rode in, but there was a light showing in the sheriff's office. Coogan, Hanning, Devon and Miss Lloyd went in while the rest of the troop stayed outside.

There was one man in the office: Deputy Sheriff Luke Mackley. He was asleep at the desk with his head resting on his arms. The light was coming from an oil-lamp hanging on the wall, and it was rather poor because the wick needed trimming and smoke had blackened the glass of the chimney. Near Mackley's elbow was an almost empty whisky bottle with a glass beside it, so it was easy enough to see why the deputy was in such a deep sleep and was not awakened by the entry of the four visitors.

Coogan put a hand on Mackley's shoulder and gave him a shake. "Wake up there! Come on, wake up!"

Mackley woke slowly. He lifted his head and gazed in a bemused kind of way at the invaders of his office, apparently finding some difficulty in getting them into focus.

"What the — "

Coogan gave him another shake to help him get his wits in order, and it seemed to do the trick.

"Okay, okay," he mumbled. "You can stop that." He looked up at Coogan, bleary-eyed. "I know you, don't I?"

"You bet you do. I was in here the other day. Coogan's the name. You know Miss Lloyd and Mr Hanning too, and I guess you know Mr Devon. Right?"

"Sure, sure." Mackley nodded his head but winced, as if it had been a mistake and had given him shooting pains in that organ. "What you want?" He glanced at the window and saw that it was dark outside. "Hell, it's the middle of the night. What you all doing here at this time?"

"Where's the sheriff?" Coogan demanded.

Mackley scratched his head and peered into the corners of the office, apparently searching for evidence of Loder's presence. Then he said: "He ain't here."

"We can see that, damn it. Where is he?"

Mackley's brain seemed to be clearing somewhat and he sounded suspicious. "What you want him for?"

"We've got some questions to ask him."

"He'll be asleep. Why not ask me?"

"All right then; here's a question for you. How did Ben Krane get free?"

"Oh, that! Well, I can tell you it wasn't my fault. I wasn't even here. They came in the night an' got him out."

"Who did?"

"The Sheene gang. Who else? He

189

was one of their boys, wasn't he? They came in an' took him an' rode away."

"Wasn't anybody here when they came?"

"Oh, yes; the sheriff was. They left him tied up like a trussed chicken. He was working late, see? On some paperwork, so he said, when they walked in."

"And I don't suppose he put up much of a fight," Coogan said sarcastically.

"Against that lot! He'd have been crazy to try it."

"Guess he would at that. He was lucky they didn't kill him anyway. They must like him. So now where can we find the man?"

"You mean you still aim to wake him up just to ask some questions?"

"Right in one. So where is he?"

Mackley looked doubtful. "I don't know as how I oughter tell you that. He wouldn't thank me,"

"But we would. While on the other hand if you refuse to co-operate we might have to use a bit of pressure. See what I mean?" Coogan had a revolver in his hand now. It had been supplied by De Quincey to replace the one that had been taken from him by Sheene's man. The rancher had also provided a Winchester and a fresh horse. "You don't really want us to get rough, do you?"

Mackley looked at the gun, and then he looked at Hanning and saw that he had one in his hand also. Devon had not bothered to draw his revolver; he just had his hand resting on the butt. Miss Lloyd seemed to be the only one who was not threatening to do him an injury.

"Okay," he said. "I can see you fellers mean business and I guess you've a right to talk things over with the sheriff if that's the way you feel. Reckon you'll find him at the Widow Grayson's. You know where that is?"

"I know," Devon said.

★ ★ ★

191

Mrs Grayson had a little house standing on its own at the southern end of the town. Devon informed Coogan as they went along that she was the widow of a gambling man who had met a sudden death after being discovered cheating in a game of poker at the Half Moon saloon. These days she scratched a living one way and another and seemed to be making a pretty good job of keeping the wolf from the door.

They hammered on that same door when they arrived at the house and kept on hammering until an upper window slid up and Sheriff Loder poked his head out. There was enough moonlight now to reveal the group of horsemen outside and he seemed none too pleased to see them.

"What in hell do you lot want?" he demanded.

"We want you," Coogan told him.

Loder peered down at him. "Who is that?"

"Coogan. Remember me?"

"Yeah, I remember. You got some

192

crust waking me up at this hour."

"So we've got some crust. You better get your clothes on and come down. You're going for a ride."

"Like hell I am! Only place I'm going right now is back to bed."

"You want us to come in and haul you out? We'll break the door down if we have to."

At that moment a woman put her head out of the window on the right of Loder's. She had long yellow hair all over the place and a pointed nose and a screeching voice.

"Don't you dare touch my door, you ruffians."

Coogan raised his hat mockingly. "If you don't want us to do it, ma'am, you'd better persuade the sheriff to come on down of his own accord. Got no quarrel with you, but the way it is we need the sheriff, we need him pronto and we mean to have him."

He saw her turn her head and speak to Loder, though he could not hear what she was saying. But she must have been urging him to do what had been demanded of him before her front door took a hammering, because when she had finished her spiel he shouted down to the horsemen gathered below:

"Okay, I'll be down in a minute. Wait there."

"We'll wait," Coogan assured him, "but not for long."

Loder pulled his head in and slammed the sash down, almost catching the widow's nose as she hastily drew back. Less than five minutes later he was dressed and unbolting the front door.

"Now," he said testily, "what's all this about?"

"It's about the Sheene gang," Coogan said.

Loder seemed startled. "What about them?"

"They've kidnapped Mr De Quincey's daughter and are holding her to ransom."

"So what am I expected to do about it?"

194

"We thought maybe you could help us to rescue her."

"Now how would I do that? You know darned well they've got a hideaway that nobody's ever managed to find a way into."

"Yes, we know that, but we think you could show us the way."

"Me? You must be crazy."

"Are you telling us you don't know it?"

"Betcher life I am."

"You're a liar, Sheriff."

"Now see here —— "

"No; you see here. You're coming with us and you can come either one of two ways: willingly or with a gun in your back. Which is it to be?"

Loder cast a look at the men sitting their horses in grim and ominous silence and he must have seen that the choice was as limited as Coogan had said it was. He answered sullenly:

"All right, Coogan, I'll come. But you'll pay for this, see if you don't."

"Maybe. Now where's your horse?"

They rode out of Pikeville with Coogan and Loder in the lead and hit the trail which Coogan and his two companions had followed a few days earlier. For the first part of the journey there was no need to ask for any directions from the sheriff and he maintained a gloomy silence. Coogan knew this was the way Sheene and his gang had come on the night when they had rescued Ben Krane because on that occasion he had seen them. Later he would need to consult Loder, but not yet.

When they came to the ford the moon was bright enough to reveal the large boulders behind which he and Hanning had made their camp and where Lois Lloyd had joined them. A lot had happened since then.

The horses' hoofs scattered water as they went splashing through the ford, and on the other side the riders continued on the trail until Coogan judged they had come to the place where the bandits had sheered off to the left and headed for the mountains. Here he called a halt and spoke to Loder.

"From here on in you're our guide. And if you know what's good for you you'll play it straight. No tricks."

"G'dammit!" Loder burst out angrily. "I don't know the way. I told you."

"Sure you told us. But it was a lie the first time and it's a lie again. You rode out this way three or four nights ago with a message for Butcher Sheene."

"I don't know what you're talking about. What message, for God's sake?"

"It was to tell him you had his man Ben Krane locked up and he'd better come and get him out. Which is just what he did. The next night."

"Sure it's what he did. But I didn't call him in. Him and his men tied me up. There was nothing I could do against that bunch."

"You didn't try, did you? Why damn it, if you hadn't been in cahoots with them they wouldn't have bothered with the rope; they'd have killed you out of hand. Now are you going to lead us to the hideout or aren't you?"

"Go to hell," Loder snarled. "I ain't leading you no place."

Coogan sighed. "That your final word?"

"You said it."

Hanning had quietly moved up to the other side of Loder and now Coogan spoke to him. "It's come to it, Matt. It has to be the hard way. Do you persuade him or do I?"

"I'll do it," Hanning said. He drew his revolver, grabbed the sheriffs left hand and shot the little finger off it.

Loder screamed. It had all been done so quickly that he had not realised what was intended until it was finished. Now he had a left hand with a thumb and three fingers and a bloody stump.

"Now," Coogan said, "will you show us the way? Because if not Matt will shoot another finger off your hand. And then another and another. Then the thumb. Then he'll start on the right hand. That so, Matt?"

"Sure thing," Hanning said. "And if we run out of fingers and thumbs there'll still be the toes. Anything to oblige." He grinned at the sheriff. "How's it feel, Mr Loder?"

Loder was moaning. "I'll bleed to death, G'dammit, I'll bleed to death."

"Not you," Coogan said. "You wouldn't want to cheat the hangman, would you? Question is, have you changed your mind? Are you going to be our guide or do we have to be really hard on you?"

Loder caved in; he was no hero and having just one finger blown off was giving him enough pain to make him very reluctant to risk having others treated in a similar manner.

"All right, all right, I'll do it."

"Well, well; looks like we jogged your memory. Nothing like the loss of a finger to do that. So now let's be on our way."

* * *

Day was breaking as they drew near the mountains. Loder's left hand was wrapped in his own neck-cloth, but blood was still seeping through and he looked a very unhappy man. He had started out with a gun-belt and a revolver; he still had the belt but Coogan had deemed it wise to relieve him of the weapon in case he got some crazy idea of using it in a somewhat unhelpful fashion. He was wearing his lawman's tin star, but in the circumstances this was something of a mockery.

There was no visible trail, but there must have been some landmarks which told Loder he was on the right track, and he showed no hesitation as they rode on; he had apparently decided that he had no alternative now but to play it straight — for the present at least.

Eventually they came to the upward slope which Coogan had previously negotiated, only with a gunny sack over his head. Later they arrived at the place where it was necessary to dismount and lead the horses; and now he was able to see that they were on a narrow rocky path that slanted away to the right as it climbed the face of the ridge and on which the horses' hoofs left scarcely any imprint of their passage. Thus they proceeded for a time with Loder in the lead, and still there was no sign of any opening in the steep rock face. Indeed, the path seemed merely to peter out where a stunted tree, rooted in a crevice, hung its leafy branches like a living curtain and appeared to bar the way to any further progress.

This appearance was, however, misleading. Loder simply parted the branches with his hand and brushed through the foliage into a narrow opening in the rock just large enough to accommodate a man and a led horse. It was from this opening that the tunnel led away and it was so situated that from lower down the ridge it was completely invisible.

Without hesitation Loder took his horse into the tunnel and Coogan followed, the rest of the company trailing along behind in single file. From this point onward Coogan would have preferred not to have the sheriff in the lead, but the tunnel was so narrow that there was now no possibility of changing places with him and the best he could do was to keep as close behind the man as possible.

Soon they were in utter darkness and Coogan called to Hanning who was immediately behind him to keep going.

"It'll be dark for quite some way. Pass the word back."

"Okay, Brad."

He heard Hanning doing so, and then the next man, and so on until the sound faded in the distance. He could tell that Loder was pressing on as fast as possible and it was easy to guess what the man had in mind. He would know that there were always two of the gang keeping watch at the inner end of the tunnel and he probably figured that if he got there well ahead of Coogan he could give them warning of what was coming and maybe foil the operation.

Coogan had in fact foreseen this possibility and it had been his intention to move Loder to the rear of the column as soon as he had revealed the entrance to the tunnel. But Loder had been too smart for him and had gone quickly ahead before he realised they were at the spot. It was the tree that had fooled him.

When daylight became visible at the inner end of the tunnel he saw that Loder had managed to gain more than twenty yards on him, so that there was no chance of catching him now before he stepped out into the open and raised the alarm. In fact Loder was so eager to give the warning that he started shouting to the sentinels even before he was visible to them.

"Hi there! Look out, boys! You're being attacked!"

A moment later he had burst out of

the tunnel still yelling his warning in a shrill excited voice like a veritable raving madman.

The men guarding the exit were instantly on the alert, and it would have been better for Loder if he had not been quite so impetuous. In his excitement the words he was uttering came out as little more than gibberish and it was doubtful whether or not the guards really caught the drift of them. They just saw a man rushing out of the tunnel waving his arms wildly and screaming at them in apparent frenzy.

Faced with this situation they reacted as any of Sheene's men might have been expected to. They shot him dead.

11

COOGAN came to an abrupt halt. Close behind him Hanning also halted. Back in the tunnel Devon and the Circle Q men stopped in some confusion; they had heard the shots but they could not be certain what was happening up ahead. Miss Lloyd, near the middle of the column, was forced to stop with the others.

"What's up?" Hanning asked.

"They've shot the sheriff," Coogan told him.

He was about a dozen yards from the exit and his revolver was in his hand. He was watching the opening for any sign of the guards, but they were staying out of sight for the present.

"Got what he asked for," Hanning said. "He's given the game away now; no chance of taking them by surprise. How many of them are there out there?"

"Two, I guess."

The sheriff was lying in full view just a few yards from the exit. His horse had followed him out and had galloped away, scared by the gunshots. It was all very silent now.

"So what do we do?" Hanning asked, keeping his voice low in order not to be heard by the men outside.

"Well, we could make a rush for it, but the opening is too narrow for more than one to get out at a time, so they could pick us off one by one."

"That's ruled out then."

"Reckon so."

They thought about it.

"Suppose," Hanning said, "we send your horse out first as a diversion, then follow up fast. They'll have their eyes on the horse and we could catch them off balance."

Coogan was doubtful. "It's risky."

"Sure it is. But we've either got to take a risk or stay cooped up here. And I don't figure you aim to do that."

"Okay," Coogan said. "We'll try it."

He checked his revolver and Hanning did the same with his. "You go left and I'll go right. Ready?"

"Ready."

"Let's go then."

He gave the horse a smack on the rump and accompanied this with an ear-splitting yell to which Hanning added his contribution. The startled horse kicked up its hoofs and went out of the tunnel like a bullet.

The two men followed close behind, separating at the exit. There was one outlaw on each side keeping watch on the tunnel, but as Hanning had predicted their attention had been diverted by the bolting horse which had been so scared that it had gone clean over the ledge outside and was now rolling helplessly down the steep slope to the floor of the valley.

The outlaw on the right was partly concealed by a spur of rock, but his head and shoulders were visible. He must have heard Coogan coming. He had a rifle and he started to bring it on to the target, but was a fraction of a second too late. Coogan shot him just below the chin, and he fell over backwards and disappeared behind the rock. Coogan advanced cautiously, gun in hand and ready for another shot if necessary; but there was no need for it; he found the outlaw lying on his back, dead as mutton.

Hanning had not been quite so lucky. His man had been quicker to withdraw his attention from the horse and look to the human threat. He saw Hanning coming; he was using a revolver and he took a pot-shot at the young man in the black outfit, but missed. Hanning was a moving target and he shot back at the outlaw while still on the move, which was no way to do accurate shooting and his bullet also failed to hit the mark. The outlaw began fanning his gun and spraying slugs in Hanning's direction. Hanning dropped to the ground and rolled over and over to avoid the lead that was being thrown at him. Nevertheless, things were looking a bit critical for him when Devon stepped out of the tunnel and terminated the outlaw's interest in the encounter with two well-directed shots from his long-barrelled six-gun.

Hanning stood up and put his own weapon back in its holster. "Thanks, Steve. That was just a shade too close for comfort." There was blood running down his left cheek.

"So he gave you a nick. How bad is it?"

Hanning probed the wound, getting blood on his fingers. "Aw, I've given myself worse injuries with a razor."

Coogan was looking down into the valley. He could see nothing of his horse, so he concluded that it had suffered no serious injury from its tumble down the slope and had galloped away. He did not have to search far for a replacement, however, because the horses belonging to the dead outlaws were tethered nearby, and it was a certainty that their former owners were not going to have any further use for them.

The ledge where the tunnel went into the ridge was not very large and it soon became crowded as the rest of the party came out into the open. Miss Lloyd was with them and she seemed concerned about the gouge which the bullet had made in Hanning's cheek. He assured her that it was nothing to worry about.

"But you could have been killed."

"True. But I wasn't, and that's the main thing."

Coogan had shifted his gaze to the head of the valley where the cluster of buildings was visible in the distance. He discerned some movement there and he drew Devon's attention to it.

"Looks like we've roused them. They'll have heard the shooting."

"Guess so."

"That damned sheriff had to muck things up."

He had hoped that the guards might have been taken by surprise and overpowered without the necessity of firing a shot. Then it would perhaps have been possible to approach the settlement without being observed, keeping to the cover of the trees. But that was out of the question now.

"Didn't do him a lot of good," Devon remarked.

"Didn't do us any good either."

"Wonder what they'll do."

"You can be sure of one thing; they won't just sit there waiting for us; they'll come out here to see what the shooting was all about."

"So what do you think we should do?"

"I think we should get ourselves off this shelf and into the wood down there. That'll give us some cover and we can wait there to see what Sheene's lot do."

It seemed as good an idea as any and they began to make their way along the path which slanted down towards the valley floor. When they were all under cover of the trees there had still been no indication of any riders coming from the settlement.

Coogan now suggested they should make their way to the shore of the lake and then move as far up the valley as they could with the trees concealing them from anyone coming down on the other side of the wood. Nobody having any better suggestion to make, they proceeded to do this, moving at a slow pace and keeping their ears open for the sound of approaching horsemen.

They had progressed in this manner for quite some distance when Coogan heard what he had been waiting for: the sound of thudding hoofs. He made a signal to the others to halt, and they came to a stop, remaining in their saddles and listening to the approach of what could only be the Sheene gang riding out in force to discover what the gunfire had been about.

The drumming of hoofs grew progressively louder, rose to a menacing thunder, swept past without a check and gradually diminished.

"Now let's go," Coogan said.

Keeping still within the shelter of the wood they began to ride at a brisk pace in the direction from which Sheene's men had come.

"You think he'll have left anyone at home?" Devon asked.

"Some maybe. But my guess is there won't be many. Judging by the sound of that lot who rode past I'd say it was pretty well the whole gang."

"And you think this is the best plan — to take the buildings and wait for them to come back?"

"Well, I'd rather be inside shooting out than on the outside shooting in. Those walls are solid stone. I'd say it's the best way."

"I guess you're right."

They came out of the trees about a hundred yards from the settlement and approached it cautiously, guns ready. They could see no one around the place, and no one challenged them as they rode into the square. Coogan reined in his horse and the others did the same, watching for any suspicious movement. There was none; the place was silent, even eerily so.

"Hell!" Coogan said. "They can't have taken everybody. Someone must have stayed to keep an eye on the girl. I'll go see."

He dismounted, tethered the horse and walked warily to the house where he knew Sheene was keeping Miss De Quincey in captivity. There was no man in the doorway. He approached from the side and peeped into the interior.

What he saw came as a shock. There was a man lying face downward on the floor with the handle of a knife protruding from his back. There was a lot of blood and he appeared to be dead. Coogan would have known it was Ben Krane even if he had not seen the bandaged forearm. So that was one more of the villains who had got what had been coming to him for a long long time.

But who had put the knife in?

And then his gaze shifted to the bed, that rough wooden contraption with the palliasse for a mattress. Two people were sitting on it and staring towards the doorway as if in dread. One of them was Marian De Quincey and the other was the woman named Rachel. The woman had her arm round the girl as though to comfort her. There was blood on the woman's right hand.

Coogan revealed himself fully by stepping over the threshold and into the room. The two on the bed seemed to sigh in unison. It was evident that they had been fearing some other person might walk in, and their relief on seeing him was manifest.

"Oh, thank God!" the woman said.

Coogan pointed at Krane's body. "It was you who killed him?"

"Yes."

"Why?"

"They left him to guard Miss De Quincey, but when the others had gone he had more than just guarding

215

in mind. I heard her screaming and I snatched up the kitchen knife and ran. He was holding her and she was struggling. He didn't even know I was there. I stuck the knife in the pig and he died real easy. Too easy for a beast like him. He deserved a lingering death, but that's the way it goes."

Coogan stirred the body with his foot. "Yes, he's dead all right."

"I'm glad. They can do what they like to me now, but I'm glad I did it. No regrets. None."

"They won't do anything to you. When they come back they're going to get a hot reception. I brought some friends with me this time. They're out there in the square."

She stared at him in disbelief. "You brought friends? But how did you find the way in?"

"It's a long story. Some other time. Point is, we're here."

"So that's what those shots were. That's why they all rode off in a hurry. I wondered."

216

Coogan spoke to the girl. "Are you okay?"

She looked pale and shocked and she was still shaking. He noticed that she avoided looking at the body on the floor. But she managed to answer the question, her voice hardly rising above a whisper.

"I'll be all right."

The woman still had an arm around her. "Sure you will, honey, sure you will."

"It'll be finished soon now," Coogan said. "Then we'll take you back to your father. He'll be glad to see you again."

She gave a faint smile. "Guess he will."

"I'll send someone to take care of you, and I'll take this out of the way." He indicated the dead man.

They both turned their heads away when he reached down and took hold of Krane's ankles to drag him outside. He hauled the body round to the side of the house and left it there and went to join the others.

In his absence Devon had given orders to the men to take up strategic positions in some of the buildings. Coogan asked Devon to send one of his party to guard Miss De Quincey and Rachel, and he suggested to Miss Lloyd that it might be a good idea if she went too.

"It may cheer them up to have another woman around."

"Maybe it will."

She went off with Devon's man, carrying her Winchester.

The minutes had been ticking away and it could not be long before Sheene and his gang, having found the dead bodies at the tunnel, realised that they had been tricked and came galloping back. Coogan saw that Devon had placed his men so that when the outlaws rode into the cluster of buildings they would be covered from various angles. If they were as impetuous as he hoped they would be it might be possible to pick off a good proportion of them with the opening fusillade.

"How many of them are there, do you reckon?" Devon asked.

"With three already accounted for I'd say fifteen or so."

"That makes the odds about even."

Coogan thought the foreman seemed none too happy about it. Possibly he was thinking that the outlaws were maybe handier with guns than the cowpunchers of the Circle Q. This point had occurred to Coogan himself, and he would have been happier if Sheriff Van Doren and his posse had been with them. But it was no use thinking about that; they had to make do with what resources they had. He just hoped that the fact that they were in the better strategic position would tip the balance in their favour. But it could turn out to be a close run thing.

He heard the drumming of the horses' hoofs before catching sight of the returning outlaws. He and Devon were in a house from the unglazed window of which they had a view of the square and the place where the beaten track that came up from the valley entered the settlement. This was where he hoped the gang would ride into the ambush.

He should have known better.

Sheene was too smart for that.

Abruptly the drumming of hoofs ceased. The horsemen had come to a halt and not one of them was yet in a position to be shot at. It was evident that they were sizing up the situation and were not going to ride blindly into a trap.

Devon swore. "Now what'll they do?"

Coogan shrugged. "We shall just have to wait and see."

They did not have to wait long. Suddenly the drumming of hoofs was audible again, but it was easy to tell that only one horse was approaching, and that one at a gallop. A moment later horse and rider came into view going hell-for-leather, the man bent low in the saddle with his chin almost touching the horse's mane. Coogan recognised him at once; it was impossible to mistake that burly figure and flamboyant garb.

"It's Mex!"

Guns were blasting off now, but the Mexican was riding like a demon and seemed to bear a charmed life.

"He's crazy," Devon said. "What does he think he's doing?"

Coogan thought he knew the answer to that: Sheene had sent this man to draw the fire and reveal where the defending guns were situated. He would have known that the Mexican was the one for the job; wild perhaps but courageous and a skilled rider; one who might revel in taking such a risk.

The Mexican came to the centre of the square where the well was. With hardly any slackening of the pace he brought the horse round in a tight turn, hoofs sliding, dust and stones scattering. Then he was riding back the way he had come, the horse's nostrils flaring, flecks of foam on the bit, legs going like pistons.

Coogan rested the barrel of his rifle

on the sill of the window, took careful aim and shot the Mexican in the chest. The Mexican fell out of saddle, his sombrero went flying and one foot caught in the stirrup. The horse never slackened its pace for an instant; it raced away, dragging the man with it, his head bumping along the hard uneven ground.

"One down," Devon said. "Nice shooting, Brad."

It was a start.

★ ★ ★

It was a while after the disappearance of the Mexican, dragged out of sight by the runaway horse, before anything else happened. Sheene could have been conferring with his men, though Coogan doubted whether he did much of that kind of thing; from his experience of the gang leader he would have said that The Butcher just gave orders and the others carried them out. No democratic principles for

222

him; just dictatorship.

It was a nervy business, waiting. There was no sound coming from the other camp, no clue to what they might be doing. Surely they were not just sitting there on their rumps, making a siege of it. Maybe they were planning to stick it out until nightfall and then move in under cover of darkness. But it was still early in the day, and somehow Coogan could not imagine Sheene having that amount of patience. The realisation that a body of men had found the way into his lair must have put him in a fury, and he would be determined to exterminate the lot of them so that they could not pass on the secret of the tunnel to anyone else. Keeping that secret was essential to him, for once it had gone he would no longer be safe from the forces of law and order. And once caught he had too many crimes to his name to have any hope of avoiding the gallows.

So he would do his utmost to kill the intruders.

The first indication that Sheene was trying a new method of attack came when a burst of firing made itself heard somewhere at the rear of the house in which Coogan and Devon were waiting.

"Now what?" Devon said.

"Looks like somebody's coming in the back way."

It was apparent to Coogan that infiltration was now the name of the game. There was not going to be any nice compact body of horsemen riding into the square and presenting themselves as targets for the hidden guns. He had doubted all along that Sheene would fall for that one, and now it was obvious that he had not. He had seen a better way of pressing his attack, knowing that every member of the gang was familiar with the paths and alleyways that ran here and there between the buildings. Instead of a frontal assault there was to be this more devious method.

Well, two could play at that game.

"I think," Coogan said, "this is where we take the fight to the enemy."

He stood his rifle in a corner of the room, drew his revolver and checked it to see that it was fully loaded.

"What're you aiming to do?" Devon asked.

"I'm going hunting."

"I'll come with you."

"Okay. But keep your eyes peeled. Don't let any of the bastards creep up on you from behind."

"I'll try not to."

Coogan moved to the doorway and peeped out. As he did so a head appeared round the corner of the building. The flash of recognition was mutual and simultaneous. It was Roper's head.

It was entirely a question of which man had the faster reactions, and in the event it was Coogan who had. The target was small, but he had done a lot of gun practice since that day when he had decided to go hunting the Sheene gang, and by dedicating himself to the business he had reached a high standard of skill in a very short time. So it was that he had shot Roper in that limited area of the head situated between the ear and the eyebrow before the outlaw had even managed to bring the barrel of his revolver on to the right line.

Roper was still in the act of falling when Devon stepped out of the doorway and ran to the corner of the house. He was just in time to see another of the gang running away. This man had probably been the back-up for Roper but had lost his appetite for the fight when his partner had been shot. Devon had no compunction about shooting a man in the back, especially one of Sheene's crew, and he did just that.

Coogan came up with him. "Smart work, Steve."

The man on the ground was still alive. He had rolled over on to his left side and was trying to aim his revolver with his right hand. Devon shot him in the head from close range and the man lost all interest in the proceedings.

"This time for keeps," Devon said.

A real cool customer, Coogan thought.

After that they went hunting.

For a time it was a regular see-saw of a fight and difficult to tell just who was winning in the maze of buildings. Then a couple of Sheene's men decided they had had enough. They got on their horses and went riding off down the valley. Hanning and one of the Circle Q hands rode after them in hot pursuit.

Three other men who had run out of shells threw their weapons down and came out from cover with their hands up, shouting that they were giving in. One of them was bleeding from a wound in the neck and another had an arm that was swinging loosely, as though a bone had been broken. Three of the cowhands were dead and two others wounded, but the outlaws had had the worst of it and there was no more fight left in them.

Coogan's first concern was to go and see if the women were all right. He was relieved to find that they were. Apparently there had been one attack on the building, but the Circle Q man, ably assisted by Lois Lloyd's Winchester, had driven the attackers off.

"Is it over?" Lois asked.

"Seems to be," Coogan told her. "Those that are left alive have either given themselves up or made a run for it."

"Thank God!" Rachel said. "Oh, thank God!"

She had good reason to feel thankful, Coogan thought. She, perhaps more than anyone else, had suffered at the hands of the Sheene gang. Now she would be able to start a new life, though nothing could make up for what was past.

Suddenly Lois said: "How about Sheene? Is he dead?"

It was an odd thing, but for the moment Coogan had completely forgotten about him, the worst villain of the lot, the head and prime driving force of that evil brood. Now the question jogged his memory and he realised that he had not caught as much as a glimpse of Sheene in the entire course of the fight, though it was a practical certainty that he had taken part in it. Nor had he seen Sheene's body or heard anyone else claim to have killed the man. So could he still be alive and kicking?

Lois was looking at him with a concerned expression, as if reading his thoughts. "You don't think he could have escaped, do you?"

Coogan shook his head. "No, it's not possible."

But he knew it was.

At that moment he heard a clatter of hoofs. He ran to the doorway and looked out just in time to see the big grey horse that Sheene always rode galloping past the well in the square. The man in the saddle was unmistakable, both from his size and the fact that he was wearing a derby hat and a blue jersey.

It was The Butcher himself, riding for his life.

12

BY the time Coogan had found his horse and set off in pursuit Sheene had opened up a useful lead. He could guess what was in the gang boss's mind; he was heading for the tunnel, no doubt confident that once out of the valley he could get clean away and save his own skin even if the rest of the villains were either dead or taken.

The idea that Sheene might yet escape justice filled Coogan with rage; this man above all had to be caught; for if he went scot-free all else would be as nothing, mere ashes in the mouth. So he urged his steed forward and the animal responded gamely. Nevertheless, the distance between it and the big grey that Coogan could see ahead of him as they tore down the valley appeared to remain just as great. Sheene was undoubtedly a heavy weight for a horse to bear, but the grey was strong and seemed to carry the burden with ease.

Soon they were approaching the slanting path which led up to the ledge outside the entrance to the tunnel, and Coogan was still two hundred yards or more behind when Sheene reached it. There was little doubt that he would be in the tunnel before Coogan could catch him, and there would be nothing to prevent him from waiting at the other end and shooting his pursuer as he came out. It was a situation in which the big man appeared to hold the trump card.

But then Coogan heard the sound of a shot, and he saw Sheene bring his horse to a sudden halt. The shot had come from the ledge, and Coogan could see a man up there looking down at Sheene. The man had a revolver in his hand, and Coogan remembered Hanning and one of the cowhands riding away in pursuit of two of the outlaws. As far as he could make out there was only one man on the ledge and by the black hat and shirt he concluded that it was Matt Hanning. He wondered what had happened to the other three. Perhaps there had been a gunfight and Hanning was the sole survivor.

There was, however, no time to think about that, for Sheene had apparently decided that his way of escape through the tunnel was effectively blocked and with no further hesitation he spurred the big grey into motion again and set off once more at breakneck speed down the valley. Hanning loosed off a few more shots at him, but the range was too great for effective work with a handgun and Sheene was unscathed.

His check had allowed Coogan to gain some ground on him and the distance between them was now down to a hundred yards or so. It remained more or less unchanged as they rapidly approached the narrower part of the valley and finally the point where the stream ran out of the lake. Here

Sheene reined in his horse, sprang from the saddle with an agility that was astonishing in so heavy a man, drew his revolver and fired at his pursuer.

The slug whistled past Coogan's left ear and he too brought his horse to a stop and quickly dismounted. Sheene fired again, but Coogan was on the move and again the bullet passed near but left him unharmed. He hauled his own revolver out and fired at Sheene. He knew he had found the mark, for Sheene uttered a cry that seemed more of anger than of pain and staggered slightly. But to Coogan's amazement he did not go down. Instead, he loosed another slug at his adversary. But Coogan moved just as Sheene's finger tightened on the trigger and again the bullet missed its target.

Sheene pressed the trigger again, but the hammer fell on a dead shell; he must have used half the cylinder before taking to his horse and now the rest had gone. He made no attempt to reload but rammed the weapon back in its holster and hesitated for a moment as if undecided what to do next.

Coogan took careful aim and steadied himself for the final shot. He had Sheene at his mercy now. He had sworn to catch the man and kill him, and now it had come to the pay-off, his finger was on the trigger and the barrel of the revolver was levelled; an instant more and this arch-villain would be wiped from the face of the earth, his reign of terror finished for ever.

And yet he hesitated. He stared at Sheene's eyes, and the odd fact was that Sheene appeared not to be looking at him but at some point beyond. And then Sheene turned and shambled away.

There was nowhere for him to go; nowhere except the tunnel into which the stream gurgled its way. And he himself had said that there was no escape down there.

"Stop!" Coogan shouted.

Sheene ignored the order. Coogan

could have shot him in the back, but he did not. Sheene went into the tunnel, staggering a little, arms dangling. He looked, Coogan thought, like a wounded bear retreating into the recesses of its lair.

Coogan holstered his gun and went in after him, knowing that this was one thing you did not do with a bear. Not if you valued your life.

The water was shallow, scarcely knee-deep, the bottom rocky and uneven, the roof so low that it was necessary to stoop. The stream made a rushing sound as it hurried on its way, tugging at Coogan's legs. He caught a glimpse of Sheene up ahead, bent almost double; but the light was poor and the farther they went into the tunnel the darker it became, so that in a little while he had lost sight of his quarry altogether.

He was aware of the danger he faced now. Sheene might halt, reload his revolver and shoot blindly into the darkness behind him, trusting to luck to guide the bullet to its mark; and in that confined space there was no telling what might happen: a direct hit, a ricochet . . . Still Coogan pressed on, accepting the risk, unwilling to let Sheene get away.

They seemed to go a long way into the darkness, the air dank and chilly, the roof of the tunnel so low in places that it was necessary almost to crawl, with no more than the head and shoulders above water. But then the tunnel became higher and wider and it was possible to stand upright again. Soon after that a faint light appeared in the distance and gradually the rocky walls became more and more clearly visible. Then once again Coogan had Sheene in view, the big man stumbling onward and not looking back; perhaps not even aware that he was being pursued.

Now it became apparent that the character of the waterway was changing; soon it had become no longer a tunnel but a narrow ravine, the steep sides of which it would have been impossible to climb, the blue sky visible overhead.

Sheene was now some fifty yards in front and still appeared to be going strongly in spite of the wound that he had taken in some part of his body. He glanced back over his shoulder, and if he had had any previous illusion that he was not being followed he could have none now. But he did not check his forward progress, apparently preferring to try to escape than stand and fight.

So the chase proceeded and Coogan felt that he was gaining a little on the big man, though he was still some distance behind when he became aware of a sound which at first he was unable to identify. But then he realised what it was; it could be nothing but a waterfall. A bend in the ravine made it impossible to see far ahead and for possibly half a minute he lost sight of Sheene. Then, however, he rounded the bend and saw that the gang boss had come to a halt.

It was not difficult to see the reason,

for at no great distance beyond the point where Sheene was standing the stream vanished in a welter of foam caused by an outcrop of rock past which the water hurried in a churning turmoil before plunging over a ledge into depths as yet invisible to Coogan.

He also halted. There was no way that Sheene could escape from him now; he was shut in by the sheer walls of the ravine and the way ahead was barred by the waterfall; he could not go forward and he could go neither to the left nor the right; he could only stay where he was or turn back. And to return would bring him face to face with his pursuer, the man who had followed him down from Wyoming, the avenger of blood.

Without haste Coogan hauled his revolver from the holster and took deliberate aim. Sheene did not move; he just stood there looking at Coogan, his barrel chest under the blue jersey heaving after the exertion of the chase. Somewhere in the tunnel he had lost his hat, and his head was a tangled thicket of red hair in which some paler threads were beginning to betray his age. His beard was dripping wet and there was a wild mad look about him. With his shoulders hunched and his arms dangling he again put Coogan in mind of a rugged bear; a bear that had been brought to bay and might be all the more dangerous for that.

"You're finished, Sheene," Coogan said. "There's no place to go now. Not for you. Your devilry is over."

Sheene gave a contemptuous laugh. "You think so? What you plannin' to do, Coogan? Come on; tell me."

"I'm going to kill you."

Sheene just laughed again. "You can't kill me. You ain't man enough."

"We'll see about that."

"Sure, we'll see."

Sheene's hand moved so fast it was scarcely possible to follow it with the eye. Coogan had seen him do that trick before, that lightning-fast draw of the gun; but this time he was ready with his own revolver and the moment Sheene made his move he squeezed the trigger.

The sound was of one shot only; not because both guns fired in the same instant but because there were still only dead shells in Sheene's weapon. Coogan had forgotten this fact, and the amazing thing was that Sheene had apparently forgotten it also; his draw had been the kind of instinctive action a man carries out automatically after long practice, without conscious thought. Maybe he had killed opponents that way a score of times, but never with a spent cylinder.

Coogan's bullet hit him in the chest. Again he staggered but did not go down. Coogan felt a shiver of superstitious dread pass through him. Was the man superhuman? Could he absorb any number of slugs and still stand up for more? In an act almost of panic he fired again, but his hand shook and he missed.

Sheene said: "I told you, son. You

can't kill me. But I'll kill you; sure's hell I will."

He dragged the big hunting-knife out of its sheath and came at Coogan, wading against the current, massive and menacing.

Coogan pressed the trigger yet again, and this time it was his gun that gave out nothing but a metallic click. In desperation he threw the weapon at Sheene's head. Sheene ducked under the missile and still came on. Coogan waited, keeping his eye on the knife. There was blood coming through the blue jersey but it seemed not to be bothering Sheene. It was uncanny, frightening.

Sheene made a sudden lunge with the knife, but Coogan was ready for it and moved aside. The lunge carried Sheene forward, almost off balance, and Coogan kicked him on the left kneecap. Sheene gave a yell of pain and dropped the knife. He clasped his injured knee, cursing. Coogan clenched his right fist and hit Sheene on the side of the jaw with all his strength. It felt as though his knuckles were broken, but Sheene just gave a shake of the head and grabbed him.

It was a real bear-hug. Coogan felt himself crushed against Sheene's chest and could not break free. Sheene's arms, pressed tightly against his injured back, were giving him hell. Sheene had lifted him off his feet and for a few moments he failed to guess what the man's intentions were. And then it dawned on him: Sheene was carrying him towards the waterfall and his purpose could only be to throw him over the brink. What lay beyond he could only guess.

He struggled to free himself from Sheene's vicelike grasp, but his arms were pinioned and the only result was to increase the agony in the lacerated flesh of his back. He could hear the rushing sound of the cascade and the stream tugged at his ankles as if eager to take him with it.

"Nearly there now," Sheene grunted,

breathing hard. "You ain't got much time left, Coogan. Any last words?"

"Damn you!" Coogan said; and he brought his right knee up hard into Sheene's crotch.

The effect was immediate and almost magical. Sheene gave another yelp of pain and the pressure of his arms slackened, allowing Coogan to slip from his grasp. They were only a few yards from the place where the stream vanished from sight, and as Coogan's feet touched the hard bed they slipped from under him and he fell face downward into the rushing foaming water.

Immediately the current seized him with a kind of joyful eagerness and he felt himself being carried along willy-nilly towards the brink. His feet went over first, then his legs. When his chest reached the edge he managed with a last despairing effort to grab a projecting rock and hang on. But with half his body dangling and the torrent tugging at it the strain on his fingers and arms was almost intolerable and he doubted whether he could hang on for long.

At this point the water was no more than a few inches deep and he was able to keep his head above the surface, but the current was stronger as the stream hurried towards the fall. He took one fearful look downwards and glimpsed some hundred feet below a pile of jagged rocks on which the torrent dashed itself in a great mass of spray and foam.

There was no hope down there.

He looked up again and saw Sheene wading towards him, grinning venomously. Sheene had found a loose boulder, possibly a foot in diameter, which he was carrying in his hands. He came to a halt five yards or so from the fall and regarded Coogan with gloating satisfaction. He spoke tauntingly.

"Still hanging on then?"

Coogan said nothing; he had no breath to spare for an exchange of pleasantries with Sheene at this juncture. And what purpose would it have served?

Sheene stood with feet wide apart, the water tugging at his legs. He was like a rock himself, as if the two bullets that had been pumped into his flesh were of no more concern to him than mere pinpricks. Coogan had a feeling of despair. How could you fight against such a man who was surely more than human?

Sheene raised the boulder above his head. "This is it, Coogan. This is check-out time for you."

Coogan needed no telling what Sheene's object was. He was going to hurl the boulder and break Coogan's last precarious hold on life. The only hope remaining was that the throw would go astray and the mass of stone would miss its target.

But even that was no real hope, for if Sheene missed with the boulder he would find another way of breaking Coogan's grasp. Or he might simply stand by and wait for the fingers

246

gripping the rock to weaken; watching in evil triumph as that tenuous hold was gradually eroded by fatigue and finally gave way.

He saw Sheene bracing himself to throw the boulder and waited for it to come rushing at him. But it never did. He heard the sharp crack of a rifle and saw Sheene drop the boulder and crumple at the knees. He had absorbed two bullets from Coogan's revolver and had come up for more, but even his giant frame had its limits and this third shot was the killer. He fell forward and the current tore at him and carried him on. As he went over the fall he almost brushed Coogan in passing; another inch to the left and they would have gone together; but that inch was vital and Red Sheene, The Butcher, fell alone.

Coogan looked towards the bend in the ravine and saw the girl with the Winchester in her hands. He could not imagine how she came to be there, but she was. He saw too that she had a lariat looped over her shoulder. She dropped the Winchester, as though now that it had done its job she had no more use for it, and she took the lariat in her hands and walked towards the fall. Twenty yards from it she halted and tossed the loop of the lariat to Coogan.

"Catch hold."

He had to let go of the rock with one hand. It was a risk, but it was one that had to be taken and he did not pause to think about it because there was no time. He grabbed the lariat and the girl braced herself and hauled at the other end. With that help he managed to get a little more of his chest on the ledge of rock over which the water was pouring; and then he was on it to the waist and he knew he was safe. He got one knee up and then the other, and he began to crawl away from the brink with the girl hauling all the time on the rope. And then a little later he was on his feet and wading towards her.

She held him for a long while. She

was weeping and he could feel her shaking. She had been cool and steady until now, but this was the reaction.

"How," he asked at last, "did you get here?"

"The same way as you did, of course. Through the tunnel."

"But how did you know?"

"I saw the two of you go in. You didn't see me, but Sheene did. I followed you down the valley. I think it was seeing me made him decide to try this tunnel."

"So you came after us?"

"Yes. I thought you might need some help."

"And how right you were. Why did you bring the lariat?"

"Because when you're going into a tunnel you know nothing about it's always as well to take a rope. In case."

Coogan looked into her eyes. She had stopped weeping but the tears still glistened there.

"Lois," he said, "I owe you an apology."

"Do you?"

"Yes. I said you'd be in the way Remember?"

"I remember?"

"I was wrong."

"Yes, you were, weren't you?"

They were still standing there with the water rushing past their legs as i impatient to get to the fall.

"Well," Coogan said, "I guess we' better be getting back to the others Are you coming with me?"

She looked at him, the ghost of smile hovering on her lips. "Do you mean for keeps?"

He thought about it for maybe two seconds. And then: "Yes. For keeps.'

"I'll settle for that," she said.

THE END